SECOND CHANCE WITH HIS ARMY DOC

CHARLOTTE HAWKES

W0011027

MILLS & BOON

Published in Great Britain 2020
by Mills & Boon, an imprint of HarperCollins*Publishers*
1 London Bridge Street, London, SE1 9GF

© 2020 Charlotte Hawkes

ISBN: 978-0-263-08808-3

MIX
Paper from
responsible sources
FSC™ C007454

This book is produced from independently certified FSC™ paper
to ensure responsible forest management.
For more information visit www.harpercollins.co.uk/green.

Printed and bound in Great Britain
by CPI Group (UK) Ltd, Croydon, CR0 4YY

Born and raised on the Wirral Peninsula in England, **Charlotte Hawkes** is mum to two intrepid boys who love her to play building block games with them, and who object loudly to the amount of time she spends on the computer. When she isn't writing—or building with blocks—she is company director for a small Anglo/French construction firm. Charlotte loves to hear from readers, and you can contact her at her website: charlotte-hawkes.com.

To Helen,
I've never walked, talked, and laughed so much.
Thank you. xx

CHAPTER ONE

IT COULDN'T BE HER. It wasn't possible.

Kane Wheeler stopped dead in the corridor of the large, city hospital that was Castleton University Teaching Hospital, and practically glowered through the glass doors to the ward. Something surged inside him. Sharp. Edgy. Altogether too dangerous.

Yet it wasn't exactly *impossible* either.

Mathilda Brigham. *Mattie.* His first and—aside from his career in the army—his *only* love.

He'd known she was a doctor, of course. The last time they'd been together—or at least the last time that Mattie had been *his*—she'd been about to go off to university to begin her dream of becoming a doctor. But that had been fourteen years ago. A lifetime.

He'd seen her twice since then, neither an occasion he cared to dwell on, though she hadn't seen him. How long had she been working here in Castleton? In a hospital that was hours away from the life she was supposed to living with her perfect earl—the man to whom she'd been married for the past four years.

That rough, unsteady thing moved through him at the thought of Mattie with...*him*, George Blakeney, but Kane fought it off. He'd learned long ago that emotions like anger—and guilt, and love, for that matter—served little purpose.

Besides, didn't Mattie deserve happiness? And if her earl made her happy, then it was better than he himself could have managed.

George Blakeney, son of a duke and from one of the wealthiest families in the area. The perfect match for the independently successful daughter of a brigadier, so far removed from a kid from a bad family in the back streets who had so very nearly ended up in juvie for a momentary lapse in judgement.

There was no bitterness in that. It was merely a fact. The kid he'd been would never have been right for a girl like Mattie, however much she'd tried to claim otherwise. And as much as he'd made a success of his life since then, it still didn't make him Earl Blakeney—a man who might as well have been handcrafted for a woman like Mathilda Brigham.

Which surely only made it all the more inconceivable that she was here, a good hundred or so miles from the vast Blakeney Estates. Not even close to Heathdale, where they'd both grown up. Mattie brought up by her loving family in the posher Lower Heathdale, and him barely dragged up, along with his two brothers, by his waster father in the lower-class town, Heathdale.

Then again… Kane gazed into the ward… Castleton was a big city with a large military population and a large RAF base down the road, from which he was due to fly out on arguably his biggest mission to date in a few days. Even though Mattie had left the army when she'd married, it would stand to reason that a teaching hospital like Castleton would value her experience and expertise and secure her for a few months. But he wouldn't have thought she'd readily have left Blakeney. Or any children.

She might have kids with him!

Kane swayed slightly, as if drunk, although he hadn't touched a drop in months. And when he did, he never over-indulged. He was always in control, anything less was unacceptable. One misjudged moment now and his career trajectory—the only thing that had mattered to him for the past fourteen years—could nosedive faster than jumping out of a plane with no parachute. But right now he felt light-headed. Dizzy. Out of control.

He leaned his hand on the doorjamb as he stared in. Not wanting to stay but unable to tear himself away. Mattie was engaged in an animated conversation with a patient. Even from a distance he could see that she was employing her own unique blend of humour, professionalism and charm to reassure and settle the patient and his wife. Indeed, the couple was looking less stressed and more bewitched as the conversation went on.

Something pulled at his mouth in spite of everything. It was so characteristically *Mattie*. He'd always known she'd be an amazing doctor, just as he'd kept up with her career as an amazing army officer—until she'd given up the latter for her marriage, that was. Being a doctor and a countess was one thing, apparently, but being a captain and a countess wasn't as widely appreciated.

Kane allowed his eyes to roam over her, as much as he knew he probably shouldn't. He didn't know whether he was looking for proof that she'd changed or evidence that she was still the same, but either way there were clues to both.

She still carried herself with a bearing he'd always admired, though her long, blonde hair, which had once tumbled down her back and over her shoulders, was now a touch darker and scooped up into a tight bun, as he suspected she had become accustomed to doing during her decade of service.

He let his eyes drop lower to the top she wore. Feminine

and pretty, yet practical and professional, it didn't cling
to the curves he knew lay beneath, but it was fitted, and
it flattered her body perfectly. And then there were the
tailored trousers that moulded themselves to the swell of
her hips and reminded him of how it had felt when those
long legs of hers had been wrapped around him, drawing
him inside her.

Dammit.

Kane slammed his fist against the wall in disgust and
swivelled on his heel to march up the mercifully deserted
corridor. He had absolutely no right to think about her
that way any more.

In fact, he was better not to think of her *at all.* The way
he'd been avoiding doing so for the last fourteen years. No,
that was a lie. But he thought he'd exorcised her, at least for
the last four years. Certainly ever since he'd stood in the
plush hotel that had hosted her wedding rehearsal dinner
and watched her on that stage with her groom-to-be, both
staring at each other with unmistakeable love in their eyes.

For one moment he had actually thought she'd spotted
him. But then she'd turned back to her husband-to-be,
reaching out to hold his arm as though he was the only
man in room. The world. A simple, instinctive gesture
that had left Kane feeling as though his very heart had
been ripped out.

He'd felt mad and sad all at once, but had also felt a
strangely bitter-sweet kind of emotion that at least Mattie
was happy, even if it couldn't be with him. Which was why
he'd left without speaking to her and without even finding Hayden—Mattie's older brother and at one time his
best friend—to ask why his old friend had invited him to
Mattie's wedding rehearsal in the first place.

Whatever the reason, seeing Mattie's obvious devoted-
ness to her fiancé had made anything else irrelevant, and

Kane had slipped out of the room before she'd even turned back to the crowd.

He'd concentrated on his life and on his army career. And whilst he was careful about his personal life, he wasn't exactly a monk. He knew of at least a couple of engaging, equally career-minded female friends who had made it clear they were interested in dating him, if he ever wanted to call them up.

'Kane?'

Kane stopped, paused, then swivelled around to stare back down the corridor to where Mattie was standing immobile, as though rooted to the spot, and ignored something that kickstarted deep in his chest.

'It *is* you,' she muttered, and even from a distance he could see the stunned expression playing over her striking features.

Suddenly his hands itched to smooth it away and he had to clench them into fists and punch them down, deep into his pockets in a very non-military way.

Thank God he wasn't in uniform.

'Hello, Matz.' The name that only *he* had ever used for her. He couldn't help himself. 'It's been a while.'

'Fourteen years.' The words were clipped, sharper.

As though it still mattered.

Kane hated it that his heart twisted in some perverse hope. Of course she didn't care, she was just surprised, even shocked, and he was just reading into it what he wanted to see. He had no idea how he managed it when so many emotions were charging through him right at this second, but he folded his arms across his chest and affected a lighter air.

'And you're still chagrined?'

'Of course not,' she answered quickly—too quickly—and her voice sounded thick.

He had to remind himself that didn't mean anything either.

And if he saw her eyebrow quirk slightly at his choice of vocabulary—using words his younger, uneducated self never would have known—then so be it. He wasn't that uncultured kid any more. He'd changed; in ways he doubted she could even imagine.

'I never thought... That is, I didn't expect...' She stopped, lifted her head and straightened her spine as if she'd given herself some kind of pep talk. 'What are you doing here, Kane?'

'Just visiting...someone.' He didn't think she'd detected the momentary hesitation when he'd stalled. Wanting, for a split second, to tell her more.

Suddenly needing to unburden to someone—he refused to admit it was only because it was *her*—that he was here visiting a former army buddy. The only other survivor of a mission gone wrong a few years back, and who was only in this hospital now because he'd let the guilt of it eat into him.

Kane slammed the shutters in his mind in an instant. He had no intention of following his old buddy down that dark path. And baring his soul to Mattie wasn't going to help anyone.

'Which ward?'

She bit her lip, her brow furrowing in a hint of irritation. It was a mannerism so painfully familiar that it caused a sharp band to tighten around his chest. Still, he was fairly certain her question had slipped out before she could check herself and it felt as though there was some comfort to be drawn from that.

Still, saying anything to her about his visit was bound to have her demanding to know how he—army-hating as he had been as a kid—had even come to sign up. And then he'd have to tell her where he'd disappeared to all those years ago. And why.

He'd have to explain himself, the colossal error of judgement he'd made, and how Mattie's own father had been the one to drop everything and rescue him. And how they'd agreed that the feisty eighteen-year-old Mattie—always scrappy despite being a couple of years younger than him—should never, *ever* know.

Oddly, a part of him actually welcomed the prospect to explain it to her after all this time. But another part—a greater part—balked at the idea. Why rake up a past that could only make her think worse of him than she'd probably thought all this time?

It wouldn't have changed anything back then, and it would change even less now. She was married, he reminded himself.

She belonged to someone else.

And he fully intended to respect that. But no one else had ever come close to knocking Mattie off that pedestal in his head. Since they'd been kids, whenever he had been around her, he'd felt his world contracting until it had been just the two of them. Which was why, if he stayed in her company too long, it would surely get harder and harder to remember the outside world.

'Good to see you, Mattie,' he said grimly, this time avoiding using his pet name for her, which had somehow felt too...*intimate*. 'I'll let you get back to work.'

And then, with the same force of will that had got him out of multiple difficult situations over the years, including one firefight in hostile territory from which not a single one of his section had been expected to escape, he turned and walked away.

'Kane. Wait.'

She hurried up the corridor before she could stop herself. Her mind was screaming for her to stop but her traitorous body wouldn't listen, intent instead on rushing headlong into her past. If the ground had opened up and sent her twisting and spinning, hurtling downwards to the centre of the earth, she couldn't have felt more shocked.

She caught up with him as he reached the double doors at the far end of the corridor. Placing her hand on his arm, she pretended she didn't feel the terrific jolt of electricity as she made him turn back to her. He stared at her fingers on his forearm but he didn't shake them off, and she couldn't seem to make herself let go.

As if she was frightened that, if she did, he would slip away from her again.

She had imagined this moment a hundred—a thousand— times over the years. She'd played it over and over in her head. She'd rehearsed what she would say until the words were honed to a shine even more impressive than that on a pair of bulled army parade boots. But at this moment her faithless mind had gone blank.

She was a doctor, an army major. She'd fought in dangerous combat zones and saved countless lives. She'd had hundreds of men and women under her command. However, right now she felt like the eighteen-year-old whose heart had just been shattered into a million tiny fragments.

And Mattie still didn't know why. She just knew that it wasn't because he'd been a couple of years older than her and so had grown tired of her, the way people—usually jealous girls in her year, though never her own family— had always warned her he would do.

She had no idea how long they stood, immobile, staring in silence at each other. Fourteen years had done nothing to diminish the effect Kane Wheeler had on her. If anything, his hold seemed to be greater than ever right at this moment. She couldn't move, couldn't talk, she couldn't even breathe.

Seeing him had been like wallop to the solar plexus. All her worst, long-buried fears had screamed up to the surface, bursting through her like an explosion of lust.

'Go back to work, Matz,' he growled eventually.

The low growl—the voice she hadn't heard in fourteen years and the only one to have ever called her by that name—spiralled through her like the hottest, deepest coil of smoke. If she hadn't been gripping his arm, she was certain that her legs would have buckled beneath her.

Mattie gritted her teeth, hating herself for her weakness, and hating Kane even more for doing it to her.

And yet…there was another chunk of her that didn't hate him at all, that had never hated him.

Kane Wheeler.

Her first love. Worse, in some respects, her *only* real love. *And wasn't that the kicker?*

Fourteen years, her fair share of boyfriends and George—her ex-fiancé, and the kindest, sweetest man she'd ever known—but, in the end, none of them had come close to prising open the death grip hold that Kane still had on her heart.

Kane. The man who hadn't even wanted her back, hadn't loved her, and who had so easily, so devastatingly, betrayed her.

All the more shameful, then, that her heart was currently hurling itself—with suicidal recklessness—into the wall of her chest, practically winding her.

'Practically a decade and a half, and that's all you have to say to me?'

'What would you like me to say?'

Scores of questions cracked through her like thunderclaps, each one echoing more loudly than the last. Mattie bit every one of them back.

'Why are you here, Kane?'

'I already answered that,' he told her calmly, and she might actually have believed him if it weren't for that hectic glitter in his all-too-familiar eyes.

Pools of deep, rich brown that actually seemed to turn black sometimes, when his emotions ran high.

Like now.

Her heart slammed forcefully against her chest wall yet again, and she pretended not to notice. Yet, despite all her internal commands to move away, her legs wilfully ignored them, and her arm refused to drop away.

'What about you, Mattie? What brings you here, so far away from where you should be?'

Where she should be?

'Do you mean on operational duty?' Mattie frowned.

She could have told him about Operation Strikethrough. About the fact that she'd been chosen out of any number of majors in the Royal Army Medical Corps to run end-to-end simulations in support of light and armoured infantry, trying new tactics for the first time since the end of the Cold War. She almost did tell him, out of sheer pride. Just as she almost told him that, at the end of the three-month exercise she would be due for promotion to Lieutenant-Colonel.

But something had stopped her.

In all likelihood, that *something* had been her memory that a row between their teenage selves about the army—and the fact that her joining up would have torn them apart—had been the last time they had ever spoken. Kane had been so anti any authority back then, including her military-orientated family. She was the daughter of a brigadier and he was the son of a man who'd fought in backroom pub brawls just for enough beer money to drink himself into a stupor every night.

In typical teenager-in-love fashion, she'd been naïve to think that their vastly different backgrounds didn't matter back then. But surely he wasn't still so entrenched in his views all this time later?

Yet whilst she wasn't afraid to tell Kane, she found that

she simply didn't want to cloud this moment with an old, long-buried disagreement. She didn't care to examine that choice in too much depth, which begged the question, *What did she want?* In the end, Mattie settled for a half-truth.

'No, I don't mean on operational duty.' His lip curled slightly in disgust. 'I mean that I thought... I *heard*...you gave up your army career.'

Her heart stopped thumping and simply...*stopped.*

He couldn't know about George. Surely?

'You...heard?' she managed, her tongue sticking uncomfortably to the roof of her mouth. 'How? From whom?'

His gaze was all too sharp. Too piercing. She couldn't breathe. Her chest was pulling so tight she was afraid it might suddenly snap.

Abruptly, he shook his head.

'Rumour.' He shrugged. 'Someone back in Lower Heathdale maybe? I really wasn't that interested.'

She wasn't sure she entirely believed him, but at least her heart was slowly thudding back into life.

'What did they say?' She barely recognised her own voice.

'You were getting married and you were leaving the army for your husband. Some earl or something.'

She made a strangled sound in her throat. They were venturing into territory she wasn't ready for.

Not yet.

'Were they lying?' he demanded.

As if her answer mattered to him.

And how she *wanted* it to matter to him. But she couldn't afford for it to matter that way because she wasn't ready to explain herself. She didn't want to make some throw-away remark as though calling it off four years ago, on the eve of her wedding to gentle, loving George, hadn't been the hardest decision she'd ever had to make.

She waited for the familiar punch of guilt that she'd always felt when she thought of her ex-fiancé but, for once, it didn't come. Instead, her body was blazing. Singing. A veritable orchestra playing with all the fanfare of the *Last Night of the Proms*. All because of the man standing right in front of her now. Which could only say something deeply worrying about herself as a woman.

'Were they lying, Mattie?' Kane ground out.

'No. They weren't lying.'

That *had* been her intention. It just hadn't happened. But she didn't say that.

'Why would you give up the career you'd dreamt of all your life for a wedding?' he demanded. 'Just because your husband is an earl?'

Without warning, he plucked her hand from his arm as if he couldn't bear her to be touching him a moment longer. Then his palm stilled as it held her fingers and he lifted her hand to examine it. Deep furrows pulled between his eyes for a fraction of a second before he quickly smoothed them out. His eyes raked over her face, leaving it feel as though a fire was raging under every inch of her skin.

'No ring?' Was it her imagination or was his voice deliberately neutral? 'Why not?'

A thousand little detonations went off inside Mattie at the unexpected contact, yet she couldn't pretend it was an intrusion. Still, it was easier to tell herself that her body was reacting out of shock, rather than anything else. Certainly not some kind of chemistry. Just as she told herself that she wasn't leaving her hand in his because she *liked* it, but rather that snatching it back would only have proved to him that he was getting under her skin.

She wasn't even sure that *she* believed her excuses.

'Not married,' she managed, at last.

The silence was so long that, for a moment, she wondered if she'd suddenly lost her hearing.

'No perfect husband?' His voice snagged over her.

Rough, like sandpaper, making her skin prickle and her voice choke up.

'No husband.'

And just like that something…*shifted* between them. She felt it with every raised, fine hair on her skin, and in every cell of her body. And she felt it in the way the air thickened around them. As if creating some bubble around her and Kane. An airwall between them and the rest of the world.

He took a step nearer to her. So close she could feel the heat seeping from his body into hers. Melting her. He dipped his head, centimetres from hers, then stopped, his warm, vaguely minty breath dancing over her skin.

He was going to kiss her and, heaven help her, she wanted him to.

'What went wrong?' he asked softly, making her blink.

What was wrong with her? He was after answers and all she could think about was kissing him. She was such an idiot.

'That's none of your business.' She sucked in a sharp breath.

What was she going to tell Kane? That she'd spent ten years thinking she'd got over him, thinking that she'd found the perfect man in George Blakeney, only for her to look up and imagine—at her damned *wedding rehearsal dinner*—that she'd seen Kane standing in that room.

As shameful as that was.

She could still remember that awful night with heartbreaking clarity. Even now, if she closed her eyes, she could remember exactly how she'd felt standing on that stage next to her future husband, a gentle sort of happiness fizzing inside her as they'd addressed their guests and looked forward to their wedding the following weekend. She recalled smiling out into the sea of loving, happy, laughing faces, all the well-wishers who had travelled so far to be with them, and how that bubble had popped in an instant the moment she'd thought she'd seen Kane standing at the back—as bleak and imposing as ever.

Worse still was the dangerous thrill that had rushed her entire body at the thought that he had finally, *finally* come back to her.

She remembered swaying. Clutching at George's arm just to stop herself from toppling off the stage. She'd turned to look at George and then back into the crowd, and in that instant Kane had disappeared. Gone up in a puff of smoke, which was apt since he'd never really been there in the first place. She'd been imagining him, conjuring him up because really, deep down, however happy she'd been with George, there had always been that cloud, hovering just in her periphery. However much she'd loved her fiancé, there had always been that little piece missing.

She'd spent fourteen years pretending otherwise, but the simple fact was that Kane Wheeler had stolen the very core of her heart years ago, and she'd never really had it to give to anyone else.

But that didn't mean she had to stand here like the gauche, helplessly-in-love teenager she'd once been. She was a successful doctor. An army major. It was time to act like it.

'You were right, Kane,' Mattie bit out. 'I should get back to work.'

'Mattie…' His voice corkscrewed around her, twisting her, bending her to his will the way he always had done.

She couldn't let him.

It was…*interesting* to see you again.' She forced herself to take a step back and break all contact. It made things a little better, though not enough for her liking.

'I'll buy you a coffee,' he announced abruptly, his tone suggesting that his brain hadn't entirely engaged with his mouth when he'd blurted out the offer, such as it was.

It was ignominious how tempted she was to agree. Had it ever been so hard to shake her head instead of nod?

'Sorry, but right now I have work to do. A long shift so I won't even be finished until the early hours.'

What did she say that for?

'Tomorrow night, then.'

She wanted to say *yes*. Oh, how she wanted to.

'Tomorrow night, I'm meeting friends. And, Hayden, it's a celebration.' *Stop waffling*, she ordered herself. Sucking in a breath, she made her brain focus. 'Thanks for the offer, though. Perhaps we'll run into each other again in another fourteen years.'

And then, before the less rational part of her brain could talk her round, she turned and left.

Walking away from Kane for the first time ever.

CHAPTER TWO

'PATIENT IS ASHLEY, a female in her thirties. Traumatic c-spine injury. Knocked off her bike at approximately eleven o'clock this morning; driver witness reported she was travelling downhill at approximately twenty miles per hour and was thrown over the handlebars, landing head first. No loss of conscious noted at the time, and when we arrived she had a GCS of fifteen out of fifteen. She's able to move her extremities and is tender to palpation over the second vertebra. She also has a fractured left clavicle.'

'Okay, thank you.' Mattie nodded.

'We also brought in her cycling helmet, which had broken into three pieces on impact.'

'Great.' Again Mattie thanked him, handing the helmet to one of her team. It could come in useful in assessing exactly how her patient had landed.

Finally, she approached the woman.

'Okay, Ashley, sweetheart. I'm Mattie, your doctor. I'm just going to check you over.' Her head, which had been crowded with thoughts of Kane only moments before, instantly cleared as she focused on her patient.

She ran through her thorough checks efficiently as her team moved around slickly, all knowing their jobs with nominal direction from her. At length she concluded her obs and stepped away to brief the ward sister in a low voice.

'Can you page Ortho, please? She's got a C2 fracture and she's unstable, so we need some portable c-spines, then get her in for CT and MRI. No evidence of intra-abdominal injury but there's a mid-shaft fracture of the left clavicle.'

The positive was that the patient's obs were stable and she seemed neurologically intact, but Mattie knew that if her patient moved, she could sever her own spine. Not to mention lose her ability even to breathe. But this was her job. It was what she loved to do, even in these circumstances.

For the next few hours Mattie concentrated on the busy A and E department. After her cyclist came a broken leg, then a cardiac arrest, a duodenal fistula, and if each one kept her brain whirling, and mercifully well away from Kane, well, so much the better.

Now, finally, she had her last patient of the shift, and one of Mattie's more unusual cases. Another female, but this one was an elderly woman with a knife embedded in her back.

Her husband hovered, stricken, at his wife's bedside. He started talking to Mattie the moment she approached them.

'I didn't mean it… I just… She was just…' He faded out as the young paramedic placed his hand on the older man's arm to calm him.

'It's all right, Vern. Let me explain to the doc, okay?'

The older man bobbed his head unhappily.

'This is Dot, eighty-two, she has a stab wound to her back with the knife still in situ. Dot and Vern were preparing veg together for their family, who are visiting tonight, when Dot tried carrying a pan of water from the sink to the hob.'

'It was heavy,' Vern added, agitated. 'Really heavy. I *told* her to leave it and wait for me.'

'I *will* explain…' the paramedic began.

Mattie moved swiftly to interject with a gentle smile.

Right now she wasn't interested in apportioning blame as much as treating her patient, but clearly the old man wanted her to understand the circumstances, and it was going to be quicker to listen than to argue.

Plus, a part of her thought it was lovely that he was caring and concerned. Once upon a time, in what felt like a lifetime ago, she'd thought that she and Kane would grow old together. Still caring for each other, like this couple did.

She'd forgotten that. So why was it there, in the forefront of her brain, right now? She thrust it away.

'It's all right, sir. Do you want to briefly tell me what happened?'

The man nodded gratefully, his shoulders sagging slightly.

'I was chopping carrots. That's my job, you see. Peeling and chopping the veg whilst Dot deals with the meat.'

'Of course.' She smiled again.

'So Dot tried to carry the pan, but she isn't as steady on her feet as she once was, you see? And she slopped a bit over the edge and onto the floor.'

'I see.' Mattie nodded encouragingly.

'So she slipped. In the water, see?' He gestured to the floor as though that might somehow better illustrate what had happened. 'And I went to catch her. See?'

'With the chopping knife still in your hand?' she asked, more for the sake of clarity than anything else.

'I never thought.' He looked distraught. 'I just wanted to catch her before she hit the floor.'

'Of course you did,' she soothed. 'Can you tell me about the knife, Vern? Was it a long knife? A serrated knife?'

'About this big...' He gestured again with his hands.

'Dot has a two-centimetre laceration on her right side, just above the iliac crest, and you can see the knife still in situ. We didn't want to turn her over because this was the position she was in when we arrived, but I'm sure there are no wounds to the front. Dot isn't on any medication, and there's no volume issues.'

'Thanks,' Mattie acknowledged. 'Vern, sir, would you like someone to bring you a tea or a coffee whilst we just check on your wife?'

A and E might be bustling, but it was going to be far easier to examine Dot if her husband wasn't hovering. Which wasn't to say that she didn't feel for him, he was clearly worried, but she could do with ten minutes with-out him there.

'All right Dot,' Mattie told her patient when Vern had finally been led across the room and her team could get on with their job. 'We're going to roll you over now, just to check there are no injuries elsewhere, and get you across to the bed. We'll be as careful as we can be, but I need you to try to stay still, all right? Good. That's good.'

Mattie glanced at her team.

'Okay, ready, steady…'

And perhaps it was the twisted way a medical mind seemed to work, looking at life in a skewed way from the rest of the world, but when she looked at the older couple—with the bizarreness of their situation juxtaposed with the sheer banality of the fact the accident had occurred when they'd simply been making a meal together in domestic harmony—all Mattie could remember was the time when she'd thought she and Kane would grow old together like this couple. And how much it had hurt when he'd walked away from her without a second thought.

Seven years of practically back-to-back tours in mul-tiple war zones, seeing atrocities that the average person couldn't even have imagined—the human body ripped apart in ways she hadn't even known it was possible to survive—and that experience still ranked as one of the worst days of her life.

Which was why, tonight she was going to meet her

friends to celebrate her upcoming promotion, and Kane Wheeler wasn't going to take up another moment inside her brain.

And if she could even pretend that was the case, she was making progress.

'My little sister, Major Mathilda Brigham, soon-to-be Lieutenant-Colonel Mathilda Brigham.' Hayden Brigham raised his glass proudly, his rich voice just about heard over the deep pulse of the music's bass line. 'To Mattie.'

'To Mattie,' the handful of close friends chorused loudly, before each taking a drink.

Tucked away as they were in a booth in the quieter part of the club, Mattie was still trying to convince herself that Kane didn't deserve another moment's thought. But it wasn't that easy. He lingered around the peripheries of her mind and if she was being entirely honest, despite her pep talk to herself earlier, she hadn't exactly been chasing him off.

And it doesn't matter how much you shake your head like that, a little voice whispered in her ear, *it isn't going to shake him off.*

It wasn't as if she'd never moved on with her life these past fourteen years—because she *had*. She'd dated, even got engaged. It was just that ultimately no other man had made her want to want to bend in her dream career as army doctor, the way that Kane had when they'd been kids.

Even George. She'd been prepared to give up the army because it had been expected of her, because she'd known that if it had been the other way around George would have given up anything for her, and possibly because she'd wanted to prove to herself that she had well and truly moved on from Kane.

In short, all the wrong reasons. Which meant her marriage to George would probably have unravelled at some point anyway, even if she hadn't seen Kane—or had imagined that she'd seen him—at her wedding rehearsal.

It also meant that she'd vowed to herself that she would never give up either part of her career for any man again. *And yet…* The encounter yesterday, and the way she'd reacted so viscerally, had only proved to her that she had never quite exorcised Kane Wheeler. Some might say she'd never had closure, others might say that she had always been looking at her youth through a rose-tinted rear-view mirror.

Either way, maybe yesterday had been her chance to knock both on the head. Maybe going for a coffee with Kane would have allowed her to see that she'd built that typical youthful first love into something far greater than it had ever really been. Maybe she'd have seen Kane in a different light—one that wasn't tinged with the adoring glow of a teenager.

And maybe she was lying to herself all over again.

'Mattie?' Hayden's concerned voice penetrated her musing. 'Everything okay?'

She blinked. Forced a smile.

'Everything's great.'

'You just wish Mum was still alive to see this? She'd have been so proud of you, Mattie.'

She swallowed hard. Her head had been so full of Kane that she hadn't even stopped to think about her mum. Her sudden death eight years ago had been so devastating to them all, but perhaps to their father most of all. He'd held it together, of course, with his proud stiff upper lip, but Mattie wouldn't have been surprised if that was where it had all started to unravel for him.

As much as he had been a brigadier, her mum had been the real rock of the family. Had trying to suppress his own grief to appear strong for her and Hayden been too much? Was that when his Alzheimer's had started?

God, but it was such a hateful disease.

She chased the moment away hastily. Nothing was going to cloud tonight. She had so many other things to be grateful for, not least a great career, a wonderful up-bringing, and a loving family. How many times had she heard them say how proud they were of her? How lucky she'd been. This promotion wasn't just hers—it belonged to all of her family for their unwavering love and support all her life.

And who cared about Kane-ruddy-Wheeler?

'Just that this promotion hasn't been announced yet, Hayd.' She leaned against her brother to be heard as she waved her hand in a mixture of pride and embarrassment. 'I have to get through the next three months running medical simulations thousands of miles away in the middle of the Canadian prairies first.'

'You say it like they're going to be just any medical simulations.' Her brother shook his head, half grinning and half grimacing. 'But you're going on Operation Strike-through, Mattie. You've no idea what I would give to go on a brand-new experimental brigade exercise like that. Especially after being deskbound for the past few months.'

'You've got Operation Ironplate,' she said placatingly, not surprised when he pulled a face.

'Three months putting in infrastructure into a new African nation is hardly the same as test-driving a new brigade tactic for the entire British Army.'

'Well, if you didn't go cutting the cords on your para-chute to save some poor kid who has passed out on his first jump, you probably wouldn't have ended up break-ing your leg.'

Then she laughed, the sheer absurdity and the sheer *Hayden*-ness of her brother's actions making her chest swell.

'I know, I'm a true hero.' He pulled a face at her before

his own grin returned. 'But you're going to have infantry and light armoured, you'll be trying out completely new tactics for the entire British Army, after thirty years of fighting using post–Cold War strategies.'

'I know. Incredible isn't it?' Mattie breathed, unable to help herself.

'And *you're* the doc chosen to run end-to-end simulations for them.' He squeezed her shoulders. 'Stressing the old medical chain until it breaks and then finding a way to rebuild it. Every major and colonel I know has been after that plum job.'

'Yeah, well, I got lucky.' Mattie wrinkled her nose as Hayden threw his arm around her shoulders.

'Nope, you've done enough tours of duty, flown out into enough war zones, and saved enough lives on the operating table, you're definitely the best man for the role.'

Mattie cast her brother a grateful look. She needed this. Her brother…and this camaraderie. To remind her that she had a good life. She didn't need Kane bursting back into it and turning it upside down. She had better things to focus on.

Like her promotion.

And her brother's respect meant a lot. As an army engineer, Hayden had been on just as many tours and been even closer to the sharp end than she had. But promotion in the Royal Army Medical Corps was different from promotion within the Royal Engineers, and she knew her brother was on track to becoming a full two-star general one day the way he was going.

'So, congratulations, Mattie.' One of her other friends reached behind Hayden and clapped her on the back. 'Can't think of any better doctor or officer to lead the medical unit.'

'Yeah, thoroughly well deserved,' another two echoed across the table.

'Thanks guys.' Mattie nodded, emotion bubbling inside her at their warmth.

Then, as the group split down to try to talk over the music, Mattie leaned to her other side to Bridget, the only one of her friends who wasn't from the military world. Bridget was a nurse, working for an NGO.

'You okay, Bea?'

'Sorry?' Bridget strained to hear.

Mattie leaned closer.

'I asked if Hayd has been looking after you?'

'Yes.' Bridget nodded, her voice so low that Mattie had almost had to lip-read rather than hear her friend over the music. 'But you didn't really have to task your brother to babysit me.'

If Mattie hadn't known better, she might have actually thought Bridget was blushing. But that was impossible—the young nurse didn't do any kind of relationship.

'I *did* have to.' Mattie pulled an apologetic face. 'We were supposed to be working together at Jukrem camp—until I got called away for this new mission. I was really hoping to be able to show you the ropes out there.'

'It doesn't matter. I need to learn to be bolder, anyway.' Bridget smiled, but Mattie could tell it was forced. 'Stronger.'

It was odd. When it came to working in war zones, or inhospitable environments, with malaria, or TB, or any one of a slew of diseases most of her colleagues wouldn't have a clue how to deal with, Bea was a wonder. Strong, confident, funny. But when it came to confidence in a social setting, like a bar or a nightclub, she seemed to press herself into the surroundings as though she wished she were some kind of chameleon.

'You're stronger than you realise, Bea,' she told her friend softly. 'You know what they say, fake it until you make it.'

'Yeah, well, I don't know how to fake it.'

'Sure you do.' Mattie laughed. 'Pretend you're that bush-veld lizard you told me about. The one that pretends it's a boogies-oogie beetle, or something like that, to frighten away prey.'

'*Oogpister beetle*,' Bea corrected automatically, but it raised a chuckle from her just as Mattie had intended. 'I don't know what I'm more impressed with—your analogy, or the fact you even remembered my story.'

'Both,' she confirmed promptly, eliciting another chuckle. 'But either way my brother will be there for any advice and support. Don't be afraid to use him.'

'Well, thanks.' Bridget flushed then shook her head. 'Anyway, enough about me. Can I get you a drink to say congratulations?'

'Actually, it's traditional for me to buy you guys the drinks since it's my promotion.' Mattie laughed, standing up and leaning over the table to address the group. 'Same again?'

She was lucky to have such good friends, Mattie thought five minutes later, standing at the busy bar and watching as the flirty bartender got her drinks. She smiled back without fully engaging. The guy was cute, and definitely giving her more than just passing banter, but she wasn't interested in some one-night stand. Her mind more focused on the new role she would be taking up in less than seventy-two hours.

The role that would lead to the biggest promotion of her career to Lieutenant-Colonel in the Royal Army Medical Corps. The culmination of everything she'd been working towards for years. The only thing that mattered in her life.

'Hello, Matz.'

Mattie didn't turn.

But she exhaled. As though she'd been holding her breath ever since their encounter the previous day. And it was useless to pretend her ears—and something wildly traitorous inside her chest—hadn't been straining for this moment ever since then.

'Has it been another fourteen years already?' she asked, but this time there was no bite to her words.

Perhaps there should have been.

She'd turned her head over her shoulder, raising her voice slightly to be heard. It was the closest she could come to bringing herself to face him without turning around.

'I couldn't wait that long,' he murmured.

Enough to send a fresh trail of goose-bumps zigzagging over her skin. None of it helped by the heat from his chest that seemed to seep into her back, spreading a warmth which she couldn't even pretend was unwelcome.

Something suspiciously like *desire* beginning to flood its way through her very veins.

'Hayden is here,' she managed, by way of distraction. 'If you want to say hi.'

'I didn't come here to talk to your brother.'

She swayed. *Dangerously.* Almost leaning back into him. This had always been Kane's power over her, and it revealed rather too much that she wasn't immune to it even now.

She would call him a loathsome man, except that *loathing* wasn't the sentiment that filled her at all. Not even close. Especially when he reached around her body to lean his hand on the bar top in front of her. And still, somehow, managed not to quite make contact.

Her body practically hummed with electricity.

'How did you know I'd be here?'

'You told me you were going to be out celebrating,' he replied, and what did it say about her that she could actually hear the shrug in his voice, even though she couldn't see him? 'This town doesn't exactly have that many places you could go.'

That much was true but, still, it made her feel good that he'd taken the effort to track her down. Her head was spinning. Did she stand her ground, or did she give into this *thing* that roared and howled inside her?

Did she give into wanting Kane?

Determined not to turn around until she knew what she was doing, Mattie forced herself to concentrate on the bartender, who was thankfully almost finished making her drinks. Although now, it seemed, she was also going to have to contend with a female bartender who, having caught one glimpse of Kane, was already sashaying over, ignoring the clamour of customers who had been waiting far, far longer.

'What can I get you?' The pretty girl simpered and sizzled, pouting in a way that Mattie knew—with perhaps a hint of envy but no real jealousy—would have made her look like a constipated duck had she herself ever had the nerve to try.

Who knew it was even possible to sound so seductive whilst still being heard over the thumping music?

'Two margaritas.' His smile was audible in his voice. And altogether too close to her ear.

A thrill rippled through her, unsolicited.

She hated it that she could conjure up that sensually crooked mouth as surely as if she'd been staring right at it. Was it any wonder that the poor bartender could barely contain her swoon? And the girl hadn't even heard the last part of Kane's words, when he'd dropped his lips to brush her ear, his low voice setting off those faithless goosebumps all over again.

'What do you say, Matz? For old times' sake?'

'I'm not drinking with you,' she muttered. Rather weakly to her own mind.

'Oh, don't worry.' Amusement laced his words. 'They use proper agave tequila and a quality agave syrup here, none of that overly sweet triple-sec stuff that you and I used to drink as kids.'

'You can't appeal to my sense of nostalgia,' she lied. 'Besides, it isn't the ingredients I object to. It's the company.'

'Liar.' He laughed. Altogether too low, and too male.

It cascaded through her. Right down to between her legs. Once she'd been the only person who could ever make Kane laugh. Who else had made him laugh in the last fourteen years?

'Is that why you can't turn around, Matz?'

And then he placed his hand lightly on her shoulder, making her pulse flutter at her neck, and it was a fight—an actual tussle between mind and body—not to let her head tilt to one side and rest her cheek against that hand.

How could he read her so easily? Know just which buttons to push? She was a successful, independent woman, who had flown into perilous combat zones and performed life-saving operations under fire. She hadn't felt these precariously jelly legs and erratically pounding chest since she'd been a teen. Yet here she was, fighting to control her own body's perfidious responses.

Fighting, but not succeeding.

In all these years she had never been able to decide between the part of her that had never wanted to see Kane again and the part of her that had fantasised about this moment. It was pathetic, really. *She* was pathetic.

So why did she feel so alive?

The male bartender finally made it over with the collection of drinks for her group, the female one following closely behind with the two Kane had ordered, and they set them all down on the bar. Mattie's brain spluttered back into life and she reached for her money, but before she could open her purse Kane reached his other arm over her shoulder and handed a note to the guy.

'No change,' he murmured discreetly as the guy tipped his head in tacit gratitude and the woman hovered for a moment before apparently accepting defeat.

Finally, *finally*, Mattie turned to face him, and it was so much worse than the previous day.

Yesterday she'd still been in shock at seeing him again. Today everything about him seemed so much...*more.*

He'd always been dark, dangerous, edgy, but now he seemed positively lethal. She had probably noticed yesterday, though it hadn't quite registered. He was unlikely to be any taller than he'd been almost a decade and a half ago, yet it seemed as though he was. He was certainly bulkier. He'd always been lean yet muscly but now he seemed to be more of a powerhouse of a man.

It suited him. As her body was only too eager to point out. She licked her lips, trying to eradicate an odd, parched sensation, and when his eyes flickered down to watch the movement, something turned round and round inside her.

'You shouldn't have paid,' she managed. 'You...'

She tailed off uncomfortably.

'I can't afford them?' he finished lightly, reading her mind far too easily. He cocked one eyebrow. 'That was a lifetime ago. I'm not that poor kid from the worst part of the estates any more.'

'No, of course not,' she conceded quickly, angry with herself for not stopping to think.

That had always been the problem with Kane. People had judged him without actually knowing. They had made assumptions. Usually, they had dismissed him. No one had ever really wanted to see a spark of decency in any kid from the Wheeler clan. The son of Mick Wheeler, a man who was feared only a little more than he was hated across affluent Lower Heathdale and struggling Heathdale town alike. And the younger brother of Richie and Robbie Wheeler, who were feared and hated across the whole damned county.

Even she had dismissed Kane, until she'd been accidentally paired up with him for a school project and had seen a different Kane Wheeler that no one else seemed to have bothered to look for. For two years they'd been inseparable. Even Hayden, initially disapproving and protective of his sister, had seen a different side to Kane.

Or at least they'd thought they had. Right up until the night her father had offered him money to leave town and never come back. And Kane had taken it.

Without even a goodbye.

Something somersaulted inside her and she told herself not to react. Not to be bitter. But then she realised it wasn't bitterness, it was pain, running along scar lines that were so deep she had forgotten they were there. And then something else unfurled inside her.

Hurt.

And shame.

She'd thought that Kane had loved her. Wholly, loyally, unconditionally. Turned out she'd been wrong.

'Kane...'

'Stop overthinking things, Matz.'

She stopped, the words evaporating on her lips.

Was she?

'Where's your group?'

'My group?'

'I presume you're not drinking all of these yourself?' He leaned over to scoop up into his large hands the collection of drinks she'd ordered. 'You get the margaritas, and I'll carry this lot over.'

'Carry them over?' she said weakly.

It was like the cogs in her brain had been frozen in position and she was desperately trying to work them loose.

Her thoughts were all over the place, skittering like a puppy on ice.

She was lurching wildly from old feelings of resentment to old feelings of...well, not *love*, of course. That would be insane. But...*lust*. Yes, that was what it was. Old-fashioned, unadulterated *lust*. Possibly with a generous dusting of nostalgia.

As ludicrous as she knew it was, it was far easier to hold onto that notion of *lust* than the truth of anything else. The truth of anything deeper. But once that proverbial seed had been sown in her head, she realised her mistake too late.

Because now her mind was running riot with a hundred other ridiculous notions.

Like how much harm could come of indulging that lust.

Just for one more night...

She tried to put on the brakes, but her thoughts were like a runaway train of carriages, with no way of halting them.

Indulging in this lust for each other would be foolhardy. Ludicrous.

Mattie knew it down to her very bones, yet all she could think was how in a matter of days her three-month posting at the Castleton University Teaching Hospital would be over and she would be beginning her three-month stint in a field hospital thousands of miles away.

So what harm could one night do?

'This is insane,' she muttered, though more to herself than to Kane.

And if he read her lips as the words were snatched away by the loud, sinuous bass of the music, he didn't respond.

She had to stop this before it started. Reaching up her hands to push him away—at least, that's what she was telling herself—Mattie watched in horror as her palms flattened against his chest. Her fingers spread out like they were blooming over him, feeling their way.

And how they revelled in what they felt.

One more moment...

Snatching her hands back abruptly, Mattie glowered at him, but for once he merely stared back at her wordlessly.

'Get the rest of the drinks, Matz,' he growled at last, and she couldn't stop a kick of triumph at the realisation that he sounded as off-kilter as she felt.

But before she could answer he turned around, with her drinks still in his large hands, and began to move through the crowd. All she could do was grab the remaining glasses from the bar and plunge in after him.

Like she always had done.

CHAPTER THREE

'ARE YOU SURE you know what you're doing?'

Mattie sucked in a breath and reminded herself that her brother was only looking out for her. Like any good brother would.

'I'm not doing anything, Hayd,' she replied, shocked at how hollow the words actually sounded. 'I haven't seen Kane for over a decade. We're just having a drink.'

She couldn't blame Hayden for his sceptical glance.

'You don't have to tell me everything, Mattie, we're not kids any more. But you don't need to lie to me either.'

She flushed, hating herself for not being able to stay cool and collected.

'I'm not lying.' Why did she sound like they were teenagers again? 'Fine, so I bumped into Kane yesterday in the hospital. But apart from that, I haven't seen him since I was eighteen.'

'Mattie…' For a moment she thought he was going to tell her something, but then stopped himself. Instead, he shrugged. 'If that's how you want to play it. It's your life, Mattie.'

Why did she get the impression that she was missing something?

'I thought you were going to tell me how stupid it would be.'

It sounded even lamer aloud than it had in her head.

'Do you need me to tell you that?' her brother asked her evenly.

'No.' *Yes.*

'More to the point, do you *want* me to tell you that?'

'No.'

And there it was. The truth—at last. She didn't want to hear Hayden tell her how stupid it would be to open herself up to Kane Wheeler again because she already knew that for herself. The simple truth was that *knowing* it didn't make her want it any less.

She needed to do this. She needed closure.

'You're right.' She forced a bright smile to her lips. 'It's my life. Just as you live your life. Speaking of which, you and Bridget seem to be getting on even better than I'd expected. She's funny, isn't she, when you get past that initial shyness?'

If she hadn't known better, she might have thought her brother actually blushed slightly. For a fraction of a moment. But that was impossible, he didn't do relationships. Or at least he'd had a few carefully chosen female companions but he didn't do *attachments*, however much they'd pushed him. Hayden was all about his career. Arguably even more than she was.

Except right now when, despite the fact that this night was about her friends taking a rare opportunity to get together and celebrate her career—this incredible promotion—the thoughts she was fighting in her brain were all centred on one man.

Kane.

The way it had been all those years ago.

Surely she ought to feel some shame that the focus and drive that had served her well these past years had faded so easily. But then Kane had always burned brighter than anything else in her world.

Hadn't that always been part of the problem?

Abruptly, she felt him there. At her side. So damned close. And she told herself that his proximity didn't have to mean a thing, but it didn't work. Because she couldn't seem to think straight.

'So how do you want this to go, Matz?'

Something darted through her. Twisting and turning as it moved. Starting fires everywhere it paused.

'I don't want this to go any particular way,' she tried, though her tongue felt too thick and too heavy in her mouth.

'Liar,' he whispered. 'You don't *want* to want it to. But that isn't the same thing.'

She hated that he was right. That he knew her so well.

And at the same time it was the thing she loved the most.

'Not here, then,' he offered instead.

It was all she could to offer a curt nod.

'Come on,' he muttered, lifting his hand to the small of her back to guide her discreetly away from the group.

She didn't even try to resist him. She just marvelled at the way her skin seared under the heat of his palm. Blasting through her. Her body soaring in a memory she'd pretended had long since died.

'Kane…' she began, finally turning when she knew they were deep enough into the crowd that her group—her brother—couldn't see them. Lost on the crowded dance floor and hidden in plain sight amongst a sea of moving bodies.

But his mouth crashed down on hers, snuffing out whatever words she'd been about to say next—not that she had any idea what they might have been. Devastating and divine. And in that instant Mattie knew she'd been toppled.

Perhaps a part of her had hoped that her memories of Kane were unrealistic, the proverbial rose-tinted glasses.

Had she almost imagined that the reality wouldn't live up to the perfect image she'd built in her mind, thereby finally releasing her from the prison of her past?

If she had, it was a fatal mistake on her part. Because Kane's kisses weren't merely hot and wild. They were scorching. Torrid. Feral. As addictive as they had always been, and she felt him everywhere.

Every square millimetre of her body was alight whilst she was practically dancing in the blaze, as though her body was coming back to life when she hadn't even realised it had been dormant all these years. A conflagration. And every wicked sweep of Kane's tongue was like a hefty slosh of gasoline on the flames.

His hands cupped her jaw as he angled his head for a better fit and Mattie found herself pressing up against him, desperate to get closer. The drag of his mouth over hers. The warm waft of his breath on her skin. It was all so wonderfully, painfully familiar.

Like coming in from the cold and finding herself somewhere warm. Somewhere *right*.

Her fingers ached as if they, too, needed to discover if that solid chest felt even better than she remembered. And a pulse blasted right through her, straight down to her core, at the memory of how it would feel when Kane touched her right *there*.

Because this madness wasn't going to stop here. Just with one kiss. This was the man she'd once loved with every fibre of her being. Every inch of her naïve teenage heart. He would be her death the way he'd always been— even if she no longer harboured ridiculous notions that he would be with her forever.

Which was why she wrapped her arms around his neck and clung on, as though he was a liferaft in this sea of heaving bodies. No one was paying remotely like any attention to them and yet, to Mattie, the entire world felt as though it had zeroed in on her. On Kane.

She had no idea how long they stayed like that. His mouth tasting hers. His tongue teasing hers. She only knew she never wanted to it to stop. But it finally did, when he wrenched his lips from hers as though it was as much a torture for him to do so as it was for her.

Somehow that simple fact helped her.

'We're getting out of here,' he growled, taking her hand in his larger one and leading her off the dance floor and to the doors, leaving her with no option than to obey.

Not that she wanted to do any such thing. She'd taken that leap now and let him kiss her. She wasn't about to look back.

'Where are we going?' she managed, a little breathlessly so it was a wonder he heard her over the music.

Either way, he barely turned.

'A hotel. There's one around the corner.'

A thrill went through her. She told herself it was just echoes of the past. The unexpectedness of the moment being just like that first time they'd ever slept together as teenagers. The bed and breakfast they'd gone to a couple of towns over. Far enough that no one would ever recognise them but not so far that they felt as though they were doing something so very wrong.

And far more special than the back seat of a car like she knew most of the girls in her class had managed. Far more magical.

But tonight wasn't about being special, Mattie reminded herself firmly as she hurried down the stairs with Kane. And these butterflies dancing dizzily in her belly weren't magical. Tonight was about finally laying those old ghosts to rest. Finally cutting those invisible ties. After that, she would be free. Able, at last, to move on with the rest of life.

And if there was a part of her that remained sceptical that she could be so clinical, well, she wasn't about to let it have a voice.

Kane used his body to pin Mattie to the wall of the hotel room the instant they tumbled inside. Her hands slid down to his backside to pull him to her, the hardest part of him against the softest part of her, and they both groaned. He plundered her mouth, again and again, revelling in every greedy little sound as her lips slid, plump and perfect beneath his touch, and her tongue scraped over his, making wordless demands of her own.

He scarcely remembered taking her hand and leading her out of that nightclub, or the way he'd had to fight with every inch of his self-control to keep his hands—and his mouth—off that lush body of hers long enough to get to them the closest hotel. One of only a couple in town, and hardly the kind of five-star resort spa to which she was probably accustomed.

But it was clean, and close. Most importantly, it had a bed.

She tugged at his shirt, hauling it roughly over his head as his fingers worked the zip at the back of her dress, then he stepped back long enough to slide it from her shoulders and let it fall, like a shimmering waterfall, to pool at her feet. Then, as she stood there in a lacy whisper of a bra and matching thong, and a pair of the sexiest heels he thought he'd ever seen, her eyes black with desire, she reached out and cupped him through his trousers.

It was all Kane could do to keep himself in check. He had no intention of embarrassing himself at the door of the hotel room.

It was years since he'd felt this out of control. Fourteen years, to be exact. The realisation should have impacted on him, but it barely registered. He had Mattie back in his arms—something he would never have believed even possible twenty-four hours ago—and right now absolutely nothing else mattered.

He pressed against her again, needing to feel her breasts against his chest, her legs wrapping around his waist. And Mattie—*his* Mattie—was only too obliging. He didn't dare speak, not convinced that his brain could even form a coherent sentence right at this moment, but it didn't matter. Words weren't necessary.

She tasted of magic. Black magic. Her light perfume—incredibly, the same one he'd bought her as a teenager—was utterly intoxicating. And it was doing...*things* to him.

Sliding his hands down her body, Kane fought to take his time reacquainting himself with her sensual curves. Touching, tasting, teasing. When she dropped her hand between them, cupping him and making him feel like he was going to go off at any moment, he caught her wrist in his fingers and lifted it to pin both her hands above her head.

'Kinky,' she teased, so that he could feel the curve of her mouth against his lips.

'Not especially,' he murmured. 'But if that's what you're after, I'm sure I could tie you to the bed whilst I lick you until you scream my name.'

Which wasn't necessarily a bad idea, Kane thought as Mattie sucked in a soft breath at the mere idea. Especially as he felt like some randy teenager again and wasn't entirely convinced he'd last too long once he slid inside her.

Matz. Mattie. *His* Mathilda.

This wasn't some random attraction. An unexpected opportunity presenting itself. This felt like coming home. The sensation moved within him as though it had been cramped up in some tiny hole for far too long, and was only now awakening from its long, self-imposed hibernation. It was stretching out, it was reaching into every corner of his being, and it was settling there as though this—here, with Mattie—was the way it was always meant to have been.

He unhooked her bra, slipping it from her, and then he bent his head to draw one perfect nipple into his mouth. Mattie gasped, arching her back, and he drew whorls over her soft skin with his tongue, up and around, taking his time, while she laced her fingers through his hair and made the sweetest sounds. And then, when he was satisfied on one side, he turned his attentions to the other.

'Kane,' she muttered at length. The undisguised *need* in her voice playing havoc with his self-control.

Slowly he lifted his head from her breast and began to make his way lower, trailing kisses down her stomach, over the creamy swell of her abdomen and lower still, until he could smell the sweet scent that was essentially *her*. And it drove him half-crazy.

Without even bothering to remove that whisper of lace, he reached down and traced her swollen, molten core. Her legs quivered instantly, and Kane loved it that she couldn't even begin to disguise her reactions to him, even as he was barely capable of reining himself in. Still, he made himself take his time, letting his calloused palms graze up the back of those smooth, shapely calves.

'Old bullet wound,' she muttered, when his fingers slowed over a long, thick, welt of a scar.

His heart stilled, caught in the crosshairs of a memory so vivid that it almost knocked him backwards. For a moment he could hear the firefight. Smell that distinct odour. Taste the sand in his mouth and his nose.

And then he squeezed his eyes closed and it was gone. He was back in the hotel room with Mattie, and that was all that mattered. He concentrated on her leg, stroking the scar almost reverently.

'Is that so?' he asked. 'Another round and you could have been killed. Makes you a hero.'

'No, I'm definitely not a hero,' she bit out harshly, despite her ragged breathing. 'We were retrieving a couple of casualties from a previously deserted village. I just got clipped getting on a heli. It was the guys who covered us in the firefight who were the real heroes.'

Kane didn't answer. At least, not with words. Instead he lifted her leg and kissed the scar. One day he would tell her the truth. That he'd been one of the guys in that village, in that firefight. Their two buddies dying in front of them and no one wanting to risk coming in so close to the enemy and during the back end of a sandstorm.

And then the heli had appeared seemingly out of nowhere, and Mattie had jumped out of the back like some kind of angel.

She'd saved more than just the casualties' lives that day.

One day, he would tell her. *Just not today.*

Pushing the memory from his mind, he continued his exploration of her body. Tracing his hands up her velvety, lean thighs, following closely with his lips, leaving a trail of feather-light kisses. Then, finally, when he could hardly make himself wait any longer, he rested her leg on his shoulder, hooked her pretty underwear to one side, and buried his head in her honeyed heat.

Finally.

And his glorious Mattie cried out, her hips moving and bucking until he had to take them in his hands and hold her steady, licking deeper into her, sucking that sensitive bud and gently grazing the soft skin with his teeth. Not hard. Just enough. Driving her—both of them—wild. She was coming apart under his mouth and he couldn't get enough of her.

'Kane… I can't…not like this…' she gasped, even as her hands gripped his shoulders as though a part of her thought to push him away but the rest of her couldn't bring herself to do any such thing.

He wanted to tell her to relax, but that would have meant lifting his head from her sweetness, and he didn't think he could stand to do that. Instead, he licked deeper, sucked harder, until her fingers were biting painfully into his muscles, until she was trembling in his hands, and until she was crying out for him.

And still he didn't stop. He didn't wait for her to come back down, he simply kept going, driving her through one orgasm and straight on to the next. This time, as she began to fall, moving hotter and wilder, he plunged first one finger inside her, and then another, propelling her on until she screamed his name and her legs buckled beneath her.

His.

And he realised he was never again going to allow her to be anyone else's.

By the time Mattie came back to herself the second time, she was already sprawled over the hotel bed and Kane was moving over her, finally naked. She reached for him instinctively.

'That was…' She shook her head, tailing off.

For over a decade she'd told herself that she was remembering Kane through the sentimental, syrupy glow of a nostalgic first love. That being with him couldn't have really been *that* spectacular. That earth-shattering.

But after this, *tonight*, there was no way she was ever going to be able to tell herself that lie again. Because nothing, *nothing* had never matched this incredible gift that Kane had just given her.

Worse, she knew now that nothing ever would.

'Mattie? Everything okay?' He paused, bracing himself above her as if he was about to stop.

She had the terrifying premonition that if he did stop, she would die.

'Everything is perfect,' she whispered, looping her hands around his neck and pulling him down to her.

And when he gathered her in his arms, rolling them both over so that she was astride Kane, with him nudging at her heat, she had the feeling that it really *was* perfect.

'I can't promise you I'll last,' he warned her grimly, making her feel more wanted than ever.

'All the more chance to do it again and again.' A soft laugh escaped her throat. 'All night if we have to.'

'I don't think one night is going to be long enough.'

It was enough to make her body soar even as a hundred new questions began to swarm in her head, but he didn't give her chance to dwell on them. Taking hold of her hips in his large hands, he shifted her until he was sliding inside her. The way she'd never thought Kane would ever do again. Hotter, tighter, and even better than everything she'd pretended not to remember all these years.

And then he began to move. In and out. A slow, lazy rhythm that seemed to pulse right through her, and for the third time that night her world began to spin. Mattie could feel herself losing her grip, and nothing had ever felt more *right.*

She flattened her hands on his chest, tipping herself forward and lodging him that bit deeper, making them both groan, loving how Kane began to move faster as though he couldn't help himself.

'Let go,' she whispered, letting her hair drop to brush over his chest the way she had so many times all those years before.

It was like flipping a switch. Without another word, Kane gripped her more tightly around her hips and began to plunge deeper as everything left in Mattie burst into bright, magnificent flames. A searing, perfect fever that seemed to consume her whole. She was splintering with every thrust, shattering into a million perfect fragments that she didn't think she would ever be able to piece back together.

And she didn't care.

All she could do was cling on for the ride, as Kane finally drove his way home.

CHAPTER FOUR

'THEY'RE COMING IN NOW, ma'am.'

'Thank you, Corporal.' Mattie acknowledged the young girl as her team looked out at the skies.

In a short while the low-flying Hercules C130 would fly by, dropping three seven-hundred-and fifty-kilogram pallet-loads of supplies by parachute. From saline drips to MRI scanners, and from stretchers to generators.

It was up to her team to retrieve the pallets, load them onto the back of an army lorry and get them back to the location they had identified for a field hospital. Then set them up for a strata one medical facility comprising an eighteen-by-twenty-four tent for one resuscitation bay, one field surgical table and one ITU bed.

The ultimate test was that the first 'test' casualties would be arriving one hour from 'drop-off' and the field hospital would have to be up and running by then. A hectic but well-organised and practised set-up that would entail full attention from the moment the pallets were parachuted in. And Mattie welcomed it.

Anything to keep her mind from wandering back to the weekend. That perfect night when it had just been Kane and herself. Even now, two days later and thousands of miles away, her body still ached deliciously. Muscles she had forgotten about reminded her of the way they had made love, over and over. Relearning each other, their shape, their feel, their taste.

They had taken their time, relearning what the other liked. Even now, she could still hear those impossibly carnal groans as she'd tightened around him.

And then she thought about when she'd knelt down in front of him in the shower later that night, the hot water running over their bodies as she'd reacquainted herself with the taste of him, the way she'd done when they'd been teenagers.

Only this time she'd had a few tricks. It was odd because she hadn't really enjoyed it with any other man. It had always felt like such a powerless, surrendering position to be in. But Kane had always been different, and she'd thrilled in those impossibly feral noises he'd made as she'd used her tongue like a weapon against him.

The way he'd stared down at her with such a black, lust-filled, carnal expression when she'd taken him into her mouth, and the way he'd reacted—like he was shaking from the inside out—when she'd grazed her teeth down his length. It had made her feel like the most powerful woman in the world to know that she was doing that to Kane, having that effect on him. She'd deliberately ignored all his warnings for her to stop until he'd been helpless to do anything but brace his hands on the wet tiles and let her have her way.

And then he'd carried her back to the bed and punished her with his all-too-clever hands and his all too wicked mouth. Taking her in every way possible, making her splinter apart so many times she'd thought she'd never be able to piece herself back together.

Or ever want to.

If there had been any way that she could have stayed with him in that hotel room forever—ignored her orders to fly out here—Mattie knew she would have done so. Willingly.

And she hated herself for it.

That night was supposed to have been about closure. Nothing more. It certainly hadn't been about picking up where they'd left off fourteen years ago. It wasn't as though he'd even *tried* to explain what had happened back then. And yet, whatever she'd tried telling herself in that nightclub about taking just one weekend to indulge in whatever that...*thing* was between her and Kane, she now feared that one weekend wasn't enough.

Three months, Mattie told herself desperately. Three months to get her head in order a few thousand miles away from home on this prairies exercise where she couldn't give in to this outrageous urge to call Kane.

And it would be all too easy to do.

His mobile number might be tucked safely in the jewellery box in her accommodation back in the UK—she hadn't wanted the temptation of bringing it out with her, focus was key for this exercise—but she had memorised it on sight. Her thirsty brain soaking it up in an instant. As though a traitorous part of her had needed more. Had needed *him*. And this time that perfidious part wasn't simply going to leave it alone or let her stuff it back in that deep, dark hole inside herself, like she'd done with it over a decade ago.

She was out here for a reason. To do a job. And she'd be damned if she didn't do the best job that she possibly could.

Fighting to tune her brain back to the present, Mattie grasped at the first conversation she could hear going on around her.

'So, we're going to be dealing with IED cases?' One of the newer members of the team was posing the question in general.

It was the distraction Mattie needed.

'IEDs, yes.' She stepped forward. 'But also routine small arms fire, indirect fire, sprained ankles, musculo-skeletal injuries. It's a bit of confidence and morale for the front-line troops that medical support isn't far away.'

'Yes, ma'am.' The young lance corporal nodded, and Mattie had to quash the urge to tell him to use her first name.

With the medical corps, consultants and surgeons working so closely alongside combat medical technicians, unlike the rest of the army they tended to have a more relaxed approach to rank in the field. But all that would be changing for her now that she was months away from promotion to Lieutenant-Colonel. Her new role would mean that she would be moving out of the field and more into training roles.

It was going to feel strange, but she was oddly excited. Or she had been until she'd started wondering how it would fit in with Kane. One thing they hadn't done at the weekend had been discuss anything personal. As though neither of them had wanted the real world to encroach on their perfect bubble for fear that old prejudices would mar the moment.

'We might even get some routine infectious diseases, which is why it's always a fine balance knowing what equipment we might need and what we can reasonably carry, as well as how long we can reasonably sustain ourselves.'

'Squeezing the most capability out of the least equipment?'

'Exactly,' Mattie agreed. 'For Operation Strikethrough, it's about testing the support network, but right now this part is for us to test our own teams, especially in the space available. This part of the exercise gives us the chance to iron out any potential problems so that when we're doing the main battlegroup roles next month we know what works at our end so that we can really test them in their new tactical approach.'

'Yes, ma'am,' the young man agreed.

'Major Brigham.'

Mattie turned as a runner raced up from behind her. 'Message from the radio-operator, you're needed back at the main field hospital at Brigade.'

'Now?' She frowned. 'We're about ready for the pallet drop.'

'Sorry, ma'am, they said it was urgent. They're sending a helicopter for you now.'

'I've got this, Mattie.' Alex, the major she had appointed to run this part of the exercise, stepped closer to her. 'You go. Shall I drive you to the landing site?'

'Dammit, I really wanted to be here for this part.'

'Yeah, that's because you've run so many of them.' He grinned. 'But now you're getting this promotion you're going to have to learn to take a step back. This hospital's going to be my baby now.'

Mattie wrinkled her nose.

'Fine, I'm going. You'll take care of it, right?'

'I learned from the best.' He laughed, then turned and headed off to brief the team.

Mattie turned to her driver and smiled.

'Okay, let's go.'

'Give me the sit-rep, Kath,' Mattie directed her second-in-command, Major Katherine McDonal, as she arrived back at the main field hospital.

'New orders from Brigade. The exercise has been going much smoother than expected. Early training has bedded in and Infantry and Light Armoured are advancing quickly. If they keep it up there's going to have to be a hiatus.'

'But Brigade want to keep up the tempo,' Mattie guessed. 'They're bringing forward the casualty scenarios?'

'Right.' Kath nodded. 'However, Amputees for Armies aren't going to be able to get out until next week, as previously planned, so they need us to come up with a few more scenarios to throw at the guys for now.'

Mattie's mind began to race. There were several medical situations she could create, but it depended what Brigade's overall picture looked like.

'Do they have anything particular in mind?'

'Possibly bringing in the Engineers for some kind of bridge collapse.' Kath shrugged. 'They're sending you a liaison from Mechanised Infantry.'

Mattie groaned.

'Oh, God, not Percy Copperhead? He's an oxygen thief. The only reason he got to Major is because his father was a divisional commander. I know it doesn't happen that often, but the guy's the epitome of the worst elements of nepotism.'

'He is,' Kath agreed. 'But I think he knows exactly what you think of him because he isn't coming in person, he's sending his company sergeant major instead.'

'I guess that's him trying to make a point and insult me.' Mattie pulled a wry face. 'But I'm guessing his CSM is the one who really runs that unit anyway. The place would fall apart if Percy was really in charge.'

'Funny you should say that...' Kath laughed '...but I had the same thought. So I asked around, and from what I can glean the guy is as solid as they come. A real straight shooter who knows his stuff. Should suit you a lot better.'

'Great. Okay, when is this guy—do we have a name?—heading in?'

'No name, but the guy's already in transit so he should be here by seventeen hundred hours.'

'That's in fifteen minutes. Brigade must really be panicking,' Mattie mused, consulting her watch. 'Okay, you crack on with what you were doing before, I'm going to see if I can't grab my first coffee of the day then have a look in Triage and the ICUs.'

'Okay, I'll know where to find you,' agreed Kath. 'Try to grab some scran as well—I'm willing to bet you haven't eaten yet.'

Mattie's stomach rumbled on cue.

'I'll see what I can do.' Mattie laughed as she left the room. 'I just hope the CSM that idiot Percy's sending me is going to live up to his apparent reputation.'

Heading down the corridor, she was about to peel off to the doors leading outside and to the mess area when a commotion at the end of the hallway caught her attention. By the looks of it, it was a gunshot wound to the chest, and as this wasn't in any of her scenarios for her own hospital, she knew it was a genuine casualty.

'What happened?' she asked, forgetting her other plans and racing towards the incident.

'Gunshot wound to the upper right quadrant of the chest from three hundred to four hundred metres. Penetrating front to back.'

Meaning that the round would have lost a significant amount of velocity before it had hit the casualty, Mattie calculated quickly.

'Combat medics describe open sucking chest wound. Used the casualty's field dressing to occlude it, as well as some other materials to hand.'

'BP?' she asked.

Good, so at least that suggested no significant loss of blood and therefore no vital organs had been hit.

'Stable. Slightly elevated pulse and breathing.'

'From the mask I'd say oxygen saturations are down?'

'Slightly.'

So probably a small hole. If it was much bigger the air would have wanted to move out of the chest wound instead of the airway and breathing would be a more serious problem. Still, she suspected the exit wound would be enlarged and jagged, experience having taught her that it was likely the bullet would have destabilised as it had penetrated the chest tissues, and therefore turned sideways slightly.

'Let's have a look and get him to CT,' Mattie instructed, taking up position on one side of the gurney and running her fingers over the tissues of the chest.

It felt like bubble wrap under the skin and seemed to confirm the pneumothorax diagnosis.

So much for her coffee and food, but this was what she loved doing. What she lived for—saving lives.

'All right, so the left side looks normal, as expected.' She eyed the monitor a short while later. 'Right side we have collapsed lung, clouding suggesting haemo-pneumothorax, and soft-tissue distortion suggesting surgical emphysema. However, there appears to be no bone damage, with the round apparently entering and exiting between the ribs, so that's good. Let's get him into surgery, shall we?'

Some wound exploration, cleaning and insertion of a tube to drain the blood and air, and reinflate the lung. Hopefully the kid should be okay. It wasn't a great thing to happen to him, but she'd seen a lot worse.

'Ma'am, the liaison from Strike Brigade arrived whilst you were in surgery.' One of the junior NCOs from Command post was waiting for her when she got out.

'Thank you, Corporal,' she acknowledged. 'Please tell him I'll be right over.'

She didn't wait for the confirmation before popping into ICU to check on her patient one more time. She would have preferred to hold on just a little longer to be sure, but it probably wasn't the best idea.

Percy would probably think she'd deliberately kept his company sergeant major waiting, but that was too bad. She wasn't here to pander to Major Copperhead's ego. Hopefully, the liaison would know that. Still, it would be better to leave her patient with her team and go and find out what new scenarios Strike Brigade wanted to put into play.

Hurrying down the labyrinth of corridors that led to the command post on the other side of the hospital, Mattie practically burst through the doors.

'Sorry to keep you waiting. Surgical emergency.'

She froze in shock.

It couldn't be. It wasn't possible.

'Ma'am, this is WO2 Wheeler, Strike Brigade liaison for the new medical scenarios. Sir, this is Major Brigham, CO of this field hospital. She'll be running the medical exercises.'

Mattie didn't speak. She didn't even move.

She couldn't.

All she could do was stand and watch as Kane rose and, after barely the briefest hint of a pause, saluted. She had no idea how she managed it but she braced in acknowledgement, still reeling.

She needed to collect herself. Get herself straight. Mattie forced herself to focus on her colleague, her tone as light as she could manage.

'Thank you, Sergeant. We'll be in my office but unless it's urgent I don't want to be disturbed.' She turned stiffly to Kane, careful to afford him the courtesy her soldiers would expect from her to do with any warrant officer and company sergeant major. 'Mr Wheeler, come through.'

Then, without waiting to see him follow, she forced her wooden legs to turn and step through the doors, concentrating on placing one foot in front of the other as she made her way down the corridor and into her office. She made her way around the desk as though it was the only thing protecting her from the enemy.

As Kane followed her in, he closed the door carefully

behind them without waiting for her to instruct him to do so. His one indication that whilst he might have followed protocol out there in front of her men, he wasn't about to in here, away from prying eyes.

And she wasn't about to pull him up over it.

'What the hell, Kane?' Mattie choked out instead, her throat constricted and painful. 'You're a WO2? In fact, you're Percy's CSM? You never once mentioned it…that night.'

Everything inside her screamed and railed but she stoutly quashed it. They couldn't afford for anyone else to hear even a raised voice, certainly not the actual subject matter.

'And you're not just Dr Brigham. You're *Major* Brigham. In fact, as I understand it, you're *Acting Colonel* Brigham, Commanding Officer for this Three Medical Regiment. You never thought to mention that.'

Vaguely she recognised that he was making some point, but she didn't know what it was. And she was too caught up in the heat flooding her body to press him. The inconvenient truth was that whilst they'd…she refused to say *made love* again and again that night, neither of them had done a whole lot of talking.

'Did you know?' she pressed instead.

'Of course I didn't know.' Kane's voice cracked through the air like a whip. Low and powerful.

'You must have,' she insisted desperately, because they were in an impossible situation and it couldn't merely be coincidence. Or fate. That felt somehow…inadequate. 'You knew I always intended to join the army as a doctor, whereas I had no idea you'd even contemplated joining the military.'

'If you're looking to lay the blame somewhere, Mattie,' he growled, 'I suggest you stop now. There is nothing to be gained by it. But, for the record, I told you I'd heard

you left the army a few years ago. I even told you that…
the day we met at the hospital.'

Oh, Lord, how she didn't want this to be happening. A
perverse part of her wanted him to tell her it was all a bad
dream, take her in his arms, and make love to her the way
he had, over and over, the previous weekend.

But she didn't want that, she reminded herself quickly.
And even if a weak part of her *did* want that, he couldn't
do it. Not here.

Not ever.

She was a major in the army, and he was a warrant
officer. He might be one of the highest-ranking, most re-
spected non-commissioned officers in the British Army,
but he was still non-commissioned. And she was commissioned.

A relationship between them simply couldn't happen.
Not if they both wanted to keep their careers in the army.

It *shouldn't* have happened that night, then.

A fresh wave of grief swelled and crested above her,
then crashed. As destructive and terrifying as the one that
had engulfed her fourteen years ago. It was all she could
do to fight not to be dragged under.

'You told me you'd heard a rumour,' she muttered
thickly.

'And you never corrected me.' He gritted his teeth. 'You
never told me you were still in.'

'I assumed you'd realised.'

And, if she was honest, she hadn't discussed it because
she hadn't wanted to resurrect an old row. It was also the
reason why she'd hadn't told him the celebration in the
nightclub had been about her promotion. She'd just been
holding her breath, expecting someone to say anything at
any moment. But they hadn't, they'd already done the con-
gratulatory part by the time Kane had arrived, and they
had just been enjoying the evening.

It had felt as though she'd managed to get away with it. Like meeting Kane that day had been *fate* and that they were meant to have that one night together.

Now she just felt guilty…and maybe a little ashamed. But why should she? It wasn't as though she could ever have anticipated that, of all people, anti-establishment Kane—the boy who had wondered time and again why she had wanted to follow in her father's footsteps—could have ended up joining the army himself.

Fourteen years ago the idea would have been preposterous to him.

In fact, it *had* been preposterous to him.

'How could I have possibly known that it mattered?' she hissed. 'You'd always known I wanted to be an army doctor—ever since we were kids it was all I ever wanted to do.'

'I know that.'

'I even remember suggesting, several times, that you could join the army yourself.' She heard the lift to her voice, as if she wasn't quite in control, but she couldn't seem to stop it. 'You always told me that it wasn't for you, that you would never want to be a soldier. I pleaded with you, Kane.'

And how she'd pleaded.

She'd been desperate for him to join up when they'd been teens. She'd wanted them to have a life together, and even though Kane had never wanted to go to university, she'd begged him time and again to speak to her father, to ask him to guide him on the way to becoming a non-graduate commissioned officer.

He'd been a bright kid at school, even if he'd been the wild kid. The rebel. He could have got good A-levels if his dad hadn't pulled him out to earn a wage, just so that the old guy had more drinking and gambling money.

But Kane had been a hard worker. Focused and trustworthy. He could even have taken night courses for those missed A-levels. Her father would have helped him.

'You told me you would never, *ever* join the military. And nothing I said ever changed your mind.'

'So I was wrong,' he clipped out curtly. 'Turns out joining the Infantry was the greatest thing I could have done.'

But she didn't miss the strange, bleak look that flashed across his eyes for a split second before it was gone.

She frowned, trying to work out what she'd seen. But she couldn't. It was like only having a few pages from a book and trying to work out what the whole thing had been about.

'How? How did it happen, Kane?'

'It isn't important.' He shot the question down with all the deadly force of a surface-to-air missile.

Shutting her out, unequivocally, and it hurt. Far more than she should let it. The ground was shifting beneath her and she struggled to try to get the conversation back onto something more solid.

'Nevertheless…' she offered weakly.

'*Nevertheless* what, Mattie?' he demanded. '*Nevertheless* I should have known that, even though you'd left your career for your new husband, you signed up again when the marriage went wrong? How could I have known?'

She blinked, the conversation moving too fast and skipping too many facts for her to follow. Her chest was aching with the effort of containing her hammering heart. It didn't help that his eyes had locked with hers, virtually rooting her to the spot.

Her mind raced back to that moment at the hospital when she'd first spoken to him again after so many years. He *had* mentioned he'd heard about her engagement when he'd told her he'd heard a rumour she was leaving the army. He *had* demanded that she confirm the rumour, but before she'd said anything more, he'd spotted her ringless finger, hadn't he? And she'd been so frantic to change the topic of conversation—before he'd realised that she hadn't married sweet George because a weak part of her had never stopped loving *him*, Kane—that she'd merely confirmed she wasn't married and moved on.

Did he really think she'd got married and then…what? Divorced?

The blood hurtled through her veins, but the thoughts in her head were still jumbled. Confused.

'You never told me, Kane, but who did you hear the rumour from?' she asked slowly, barely recognising her own voice.

He stopped, his eyes catching hers, refusing to let them slide away. Pinning her where she stood. The silence in the room so tense it almost suffocated her. And all she could do was wait.

'You,' he said eventually. 'I heard from you when you announced that you were leaving to concentrate on being a civilian doctor.'

Mattie didn't answer, she merely shook her head adamantly. But the hammering was making its way into her brain, pressing on her temples. There was only one time she could think of that she'd made any such kind of public statement.

'What do you mean, *I announced it*?' she asked carefully.

His face shuttered down. Effectively locking her out.

'Forget I said anything.'

She knew this side of Kane. This so-called stubborn streak that people had always taken to mean that, once he'd taken a stand, there was no talking him around. But Mattie also knew that it was less about blind stubbornness and more about trying to protect himself.

And with an upbringing like his, he'd needed to protect himself from a lot.

Nonetheless, her legs were still threatening to skitter away from underneath her. Very un-major-like. Certainly uncharacteristic. She didn't know how, but Mattie drew herself up to her full five-foot-seven height. It might have worked had Kane not been a full eight inches taller. She still had to tilt her head up towards him, which did nothing to lessen the aura of power that swirled around him.

'You were there,' she whispered at last. 'At my wedding rehearsal. Weren't you?'

How did her voice sound so...*normal* when her tongue felt too thick, too heavy for her own mouth?

'I thought I saw you,' she pressed on when Kane didn't answer. 'But then...you were gone.'

He still didn't answer, and the silence pulled between then, taut and close. She tried again.

'I thought I'd imagined you.'

Still he didn't react, and Mattie hated it that she couldn't read him. That she had no idea what he was thinking.

How could she bring herself to tell him the rest, if she didn't know what was going on in that closed-off head of his? How could she admit that she'd called off the wedding to George because she'd finally accepted the fact that no one else would ever claim her heart whilst it had still been trying to cling to the memory of Kane?

She needed something from him. Anything.

'Why didn't you say something, Kane? Anything?' She could hear her voice rising and she fought to pull it back under control. 'What were you even doing there?'

'What does it even matter now?' he demanded, his voice too gritty, too raw for her to bear. 'You married him, and it fell apart. You moved on. It happens.'

'It *doesn't* happen,' she choked out. 'At least, not like that.'

'I'm not entirely sure I understand what you're saying.'

He lifted his shoulders, as if it didn't matter one way or the other.

But it *did* matter. At least, to her. He stared at her and she shook her head, searching for the right words.

'My marriage didn't fall apart,' she choked out at last. 'My engagement did.'

Another icy fog of silence swirled around the room. Mattie tried not to shiver, but it was hopeless.

'Say again?' Kane rasped eventually.

She didn't think she could until she heard the words dropping awkwardly from her lips. 'I never left the army because I never married. I called it off after that night... after the wedding rehearsal.'

'Why?'

She'd known the question was coming but she couldn't bring herself to answer it. How could she tell him the truth? What would be the point?

Because when it had come down to it, the only reason her marriage to dear, sweet, kind George—who had to have been the most perfect man alive—had fallen apart was simply because he hadn't been Kane.

As shameful as that was.

And now that they were in the situation they were in... what difference did it make anyway?

CHAPTER FIVE

MATTIE WASN'T JUST not married *to her precious earl...she'd* never *married him.*

The revelation rolled round and round in Kane's head until he couldn't think of anything else. He wasn't even sure that he was still breathing.

And she *had* seen him that night after all. He hadn't just imagined her staring right at him. But all this while that he'd told himself she'd turned to her fiancé without even appearing to take a second look in his direction—effectively dismissing him from her thoughts, her life—the reality was that she'd thought she'd simply imagined him.

What the hell was he supposed to take from that?

The fact that Mattie had accepted the idea that her subconscious had conjured up an image of her first boyfriend on the night of her wedding rehearsal dinner. And the fact that she had ended up not going through with her wedding. Those two thoughts raced through Kane's head, so utterly neck and neck that he couldn't tell which thought was chasing the other. Or even if they were connected at all.

Questions jostled for room in his head, elbowing each other out of the way as they tried to get to his tongue. To spill out into the silence. But Kane didn't want to let them. He needed time to absorb this new revelation. He needed to think.

Mattie, it seemed, had other ideas.

'How did you know I was getting married?' she demanded, and he tried not to read too much into the breathless tone. 'How did you even get inside? It was a private party.'

He had no intention of replying so it was something of a shock when he heard the words leave his own mouth, as gravelly as his voice sounded.

'Hayd contacted me.'

She stared at him for a long moment.

'My brother invited you?'

Had it been an invitation as such?

He'd never really thought about it, preferring to shut the whole incident from his mind.

'He told me you were getting married,' Kane offered evenly. 'And he told me that he was going to the rehearsal dinner at the hotel.'

'I didn't even know you two were in contact. He never told me.' She sounded annoyed and distraught all at the same time. 'He never even mentioned you to me.'

Kane didn't answer. He didn't know how to. How was he supposed to tell Mattie that Hayden's call had come out of the blue? That he hadn't spoken to her brother, or indeed had any contact with Hayden since the night Kane had walked away from the Brigham family—from Mattie—for good?

'We weren't in contact.'

'You must have been.' She shook her head, clearly trying to make sense out of it.

He wished she could. He'd been trying to, and failing, for the past four years.

'I had no contact with Hayden either before or after. Just that one call. One time. Maybe he thought I'd talk to you, I don't know. I just know that when I saw you there, looking so happy, I left. And I never heard from your brother again.'

And had then spent four years pretending he wasn't kicking himself for not doing more. Pretending that he hadn't tormented himself with what-ifs. A thing he worked hard never to do in any other area of his life.

A part of him had harboured the idea that maybe Mattie's father had played some part in getting his son to contact Kane and alert him to the wedding. After all, he was the only one of the Brigham family who had known where Kane had gone. And why. Without Mattie's father's help, he would never be where he was now.

The high-ranking officer hadn't pulled strings, of course, he had always had far too much integrity for that. He'd merely opened doors for Kane that would otherwise have remained firmly locked. It had then been up to Kane himself to walk through them and prove he was worth talking to.

But he couldn't explain any of that to Mattie. Not just because he didn't want to drop a bombshell that although she'd clearly had no idea where he'd been these past fourteen years, her father *had* known. But also because he was still ashamed of the actions that had led to him leaving without warning in the first place.

Anyway, she wasn't asking about what had happened fourteen years ago, but was asking how he'd come to be at her wedding rehearsal four years ago. And he wasn't sure he could give her the answer she wanted. Even to him—and even though he couldn't make sense of *why*— it sounded as though Hayden hadn't wanted his sister to marry her Earl Blakeney.

'I don't have the answers you want, Mattie,' Kane managed, wondering how he didn't burst into flames at the sheer effort of shutting it down. Especially since he desperately wanted to have that conversation, too.

'But we're not here to rake over our past personal life. We're here for Operation Strikethrough. So that you can set up the medical scenarios that will test our infantry platoons to their limits.'

He could see the emotions buffeting Mattie. The same emotions that were tearing through him. But he couldn't let them in. He *wouldn't*. It would serve no purpose now, too much time had passed.

'So we're just going to…what? Pretend the other night didn't happen?' Sharpness pierced her tone, striking him.

He had no idea how he pretended it didn't score a direct hit.

'I don't see what choice we have, Mattie.' It took everything in him to keep his tone neutral. Distant. 'I'm a warrant officer, you're a major. I've led seminars on what would happen if any of my NCOs were caught having a relationship with a commissioned officer, even a colour sergeant with a lieutenant. You know what would happen if they discovered anything between you and me.'

'You don't have to remind me.' She straightened her shoulders. 'I'm well aware. One or both of us would lose our careers. I *have* briefed my own share of subbies on the consequences of fraternisation with privates or NCOs.'

'Even if anyone found out about what happened between us at the weekend—which they won't, of course, but even if they did—there could be no fallout.'

They hadn't known the situation then. They'd had no idea the other was also in the military. But they did now.

'It just can't happen, Mattie.' He didn't know whether he was trying to convince her or himself.

'It wasn't going to,' she snorted.

But he could tell she was lying, though it gave him little comfort.

'Then surely that's all the more reason to lock it away and pretend it didn't happen, don't you think?' No reason for her to know that he had to bite every unpalatable word out. 'What's the point in dissecting it further?'

She glared at him and never before had he so fervently wished he could read what was going on behind those deep pools of hazel.

'No point at all,' she clipped out at length. 'You're right. We just need to get through the next couple of days and then…'

'Then?' he prompted, when she appeared to falter.

She squared her shoulders and her black gaze jolted through him, leaving him feeling even more wretched than ever.

'Then I don't imagine we'll cross paths again,' she managed. 'You're infantry, I'm medical. After all, we haven't until now.'

Something slithered and twisted through him but he refused to acknowledge it. He dipped his head instead, his voice even.

'I don't imagine we will.' And even though it scraped against everything else he wanted to say, he pushed past it.

Neither of them spoke, each lost in their own thoughts.

'So, that day back at the hospital…' Mattie broke the silence suddenly. 'You said you were visiting someone. I assumed it was a patient in the main hospital, but I'm guessing now it was someone in the military wing.'

He hesitated, weighing up what to tell her. What harm could it do?

'One of my former men,' Kane confirmed after a moment. 'He was also a buddy. My OC was hardly going to make the trip, even though it was about ten minutes from barracks, so I thought I would.'

'Major Percy Copperhead?' She pulled a face, though he doubted she'd intended to. 'He's an idiot.'

At least he wasn't alone in his distaste for the man.

'He is,' Kane concurred. 'In fourteen years I've known a few idiots—there are plenty of good officers, don't get me wrong, but a couple of bad ones. Copperhead takes the prize, though.'

'At least it isn't just me, then.' Mattie forced an awkward laugh. 'So you've been in the army for fourteen years?'

From the moment he'd walked away from their relationship without even a goodbye.

Kane didn't need to hear the words aloud to recognise the unspoken question in her tone.

She was piecing it together yet he couldn't answer her. He *wouldn't.* Because that would mean diving into a part of his past he was still desperate to keep locked away. He was still so ashamed that he wanted to pretend that it had never happened. Even with Mattie.

Especially with Mattie.

So, instead, he picked out a document from his folder and turned to the third page.

And he certainly wasn't about to let her know that it damned near killed him to do so.

'I assume you read our original brief?'

For a fraction of a moment he thought she blinked, but then it was gone and she was making her way around her desk to locate the files.

'Outlining the medical scenarios the division wants to test? Yes, originally there were two parts to it, the first one being individual scenarios testing the combat medical guys.'

'Right. The second exercise is more a front-line exercise, role one support with mass casualties. Setting up a medical search team to follow the infantry in, we had a FIBUA location in mind.'

They both knew that training for fire fights in built up, urban areas, was essential, so he could understand Mattie's frown.

'Had?'

'Depending on how the main operation is progressing,

there's a chance we have to bring forward that scenario, which would mean choosing a new location. From our POV that scenario will be a chance to look at command and control aspects.'

'So plenty of casualties, a tactical environment, with your guys under pressure,' Mattie confirmed. 'From our perspective it will be more about seeing the medical treatment the medics can provide and we've got about one hundred and forty medics taking part.'

'For a lot of these guys it will be the first chance they'll have had to see real-life amputees made up to look like the accidents have just happened. We've got another infantry unit coming in to keep them under constant fire to really ramp up that pressure. It's going to be about making sure they can keep calm and seeing how fast they can select a good building in which to set up medical treatment facilities.

'And stressing the new tactical set-up?' Mattie surmised.

Kane bowed his head.

'Right.'

'Okay, so all of that seems as expected as we'd planned for them next week, using exercise casualties from this hospital. Amputees for Armies are being flown in next week, and we have HFMSs, high-fidelity mannequin simulators.'

'I'm familiar with them,' he confirmed. 'Full-size dummies, computer controlled, which you'll make up to look like injured soldiers—even those caught by IEDs or mines and losing limbs.'

'They can recreate physiological issues such as blood pressure, heart rate, breathing, as well as normal and abnormal heart sounds, lung sounds and pupil findings,' Mattie continued, clearly beginning to find her feet now they'd moved away from the personal and into the medical side of the operation.

It was ridiculous that he couldn't seem to do the same. Couldn't stop his eyes from wandering to her lips and remembering how soft and plump they felt. Or following the sweet curve of her neck and recall how she'd quivered in his arms when he'd kissed that sensitive hollow by her collarbone.

Not to mention the primal, caveman part of himself that was barely containing itself from stripping her and throwing her on her desk, hearing her scream his name again as he buried his head in the sweet heat between her legs.

The way he'd promised himself he would do the moment this exercise was over, when he'd thought all he had to do was return to the hospital and find her there, waiting for him.

When he'd planned to tell her everything.

'The mannequins can vary blood pressure, heart rate and breathing, and many of them can simulate going into cardiac arrest,' she continued, oblivious to his wild, uncontrollable thoughts. 'Depending on how far you want to test your different level of medics at section level, platoon level or company level, HFMSs can even respond to medication and oxygen administration, receiving electrical cardioversion and procedures such as diagnostic peritoneal lavage and central lines.'

'Okay.' Moving forward, Kane tried to get a grip of his wayward thoughts and settled in front of the large map on the pinboard on the side wall of the room.

He did it more to move away from her than because he needed to. Because if she got any closer he knew he would smell that familiar, vanilla scent of her hair, as tightly scraped back in that bun as it was. And his fingers were already itching with the desire to pull it free and tunnel his fingers into its luxurious silkiness.

'So,' he managed, 'to summarise, we can't get the Amputees for Armies flown in any earlier than scheduled, but we should be able to use the HFMSs and your guys made up to look like casualties. I suggest we go through each potential scenario one at a time, decide on what can best be gained by it, and then feed it into a new time and grid reference.'

'Fine.' Mattie whipped through the pages, annotated with her own notes, before standing up and moving to join him at the board. 'Starting with the incident on page four, where you've highlighted a bridge collapse.'

He sidestepped again. Like a besotted teenager next to their crush. It might have even been comical, if it wasn't so damned tragic.

'Yeah.' He coughed brusquely. 'We're looking at setting up a tank fall so the Engineers can have a play with their toys.'

'How about if we use it to introduce a crush scenario? We can have a two-stage approach, with stage one concentrating on your medics and soldiers in the field, right up to extraction using one of our MERT helicopters. Stage two will be for us back at the field hospital.'

The Medical Emergency Response Team were always an essential part of any operation, as was the field hospital.

'Okay.' Kane nodded, taking his own notes. 'I'm aware that there are arguments and recommendations for leaving crush victims in situ if they have been trapped for more than fifteen minutes, but on the other hand there's an argument concerning crush syndrome for releasing them as soon as possible.'

'Yes, so let me explain,' she began, her evident passion for her work making him smile despite everything.

He cocked an eyebrow at her.

'In layman's terms, Mattie,' he cautioned.

At least she had the grace to flush. But that only made

him wonder if the stain was spreading down her deliciously creamy chest. To the gentle swells that he ached to touch again.

To taste them again.

'Right. Of course. When the human body is crushed, in this instance between a vehicle and a bridge deck, it is subjected to pressure. Muscular compression damages the muscle cells and leads to a process called rhabdomyolysis.' She eyed him briefly before hastily skating over the explanation he knew she'd been about to give him.

If he didn't know better, he'd say she was talking for the sake of it. That, in reality, she was finding this conversation as distracting as he was. And he could have sworn her breathing was a little shallower than it had been. A little more rapid.

'Okay, the point is that rhabdomyolysis causes organ dysfunction such as acute renal failure, so the likelihood of developing acute crush syndrome is directly related to the length of time the body is under compression.'

'So you're looking for the guys to release the victim or victims as soon as possible,' Kane surmised, his brain clouding over as she shifted, subconsciously, closer to him.

'Irrespective of how long they've been trapped.' She nodded a little jerkily. 'But they will need to apply tourniquets.'

'Right.' It was impossible to concentrate when he felt her in every part of himself, like this.

'Your guys will need to administer pain relief. I know they'll each have the lollipop lozenges with fentanyl, but in this instance you're going to need the section medic to administer a strong intramuscular morphine shot.'

Everything was falling away. Her office. The hospital, even the fact that they were on a military training ground. There was only Mattie.

'Testing that long flight scenario requiring inflight operation on the MERT, I would put with a forward unit, so arguably this location here.' He pointed to the map, indicating the grid reference.

His hadn't intended it—at least, not on any conscious level—but his hand brushed hers as he moved.

He might as well have self-combusted.

'Agreed.' She swallowed. Hard. 'I'll send a couple of Directing Staff there on your instruction. And the veterans who have already suffered life-changing injuries will act as serious casualties for the simulations.'

There was a roar in his head. A rushing noise, drowning out everything else. He fought to maintain some semblance of restraint, but she was leaning into him now. Her warmth, her scent were irresistible.

'Yeah, once they fly in, your medical staff who aren't on the exercise can decide how best to make them up.'

His voice cracked, but she didn't notice. She was too intent on staring at him, her voice growing softer, murmuring the words as if on autopilot.

'Multiple casualties, some big pyrotechnics to make the scenarios as realistic as possible.'

Kane snaked out his hand and slid it around the back of her neck, tugging her to him. She didn't even pretend to resist, her hands circling his upper arms, her papers floating to the floor with a soft swishing noise.

The kiss was hotter, and wilder, than even he had remembered. Carnal, feral, savage. He ravaged her mouth with his own, dragging his tongue across her lips, dipping into her mouth then out again. And she met him stroke for stroke. Like she was caught up in the same madness that was sweeping him away. He kissed her, over and over, plundering and demanding. Imagining that somehow, some way these kisses branded her and made her *his*.

And then he was scooping her up, his hands holding her backside as she wrapped her legs around him. He carried her to the desk, his mouth never leaving hers. The heat from her body, so hot and inviting, even through their clothing, was making the blood roar in his ears. Making him want to taste her again, just like the other night. He reached down between them and ran his fingers up the seam of her trousers, right where she was molten for him, and the soft, greedy sound she emitted made him ache almost painfully.

He wasn't prepared for her to tear her mouth from his.

'Wait.' Her breathing was ragged, wrecked. And Kane found that he liked that rather too much.

But, still, he wasn't sure he could wait at all. He moved his hand and ran it over her core again, and her eyelids fluttered down as she bit her lip.

God, but she was beautiful.

And then she drew back, sliding her hands over his arms, as if testing out the muscles, and then she moved them to his chest, letting her palms glide down his pectorals, his abs, until she was suddenly cupping his sex, sliding down the zip of his trousers without preamble and slipping her hand inside.

'I rather think, Kane,' she told him, in the sexiest, most commanding voice he thought he'd ever heard, 'that you took charge last time. Now it's my turn.'

Before he could speak, her hot fingers closed around him, applying just the right amount of pressure, and then moving up, down *so damn slowly.* He bit back a deep groan. It had to be the most perfect torture he'd ever known in his life. She was taking charge, as though she couldn't wait another moment to touch him, to taste him, to do whatever it was that she wanted to do to him. And he feared he might let her. Right here and now.

What was it about this one woman that had him—had always had him—so crazy and unbridled?

He pulled her body to his and she fitted against him like

she always did. Like she always *had.* Kane forgot what the rules were, what he could do, and what he couldn't. He forgot that this couldn't happen. He simply knew that wanted her with every fibre of his being, and what was even more incredible was that she wanted him, too.

A loud knock on the door jarred them both back to reality.

As Mattie sprang backwards, he kept his back to the door, aware that his body was a giveaway sign of what had just been happening.

'I'm sorry to disturb you, Major Brigham,' the voice began, 'but ICU called to say your gunshot patient has developed complications, and you might want to see him.'

It was like a switch being pushed in her, Kane noted as she acknowledged the corporal before turning back to him.

'I really do have to go and attend this.' A statement, not a question. 'I'm sure Mr Wheeler has a couple of notes he wants to finish up here for now, but if you wait outside, Corporal, perhaps you can escort him to the mess hall for something to eat or drink whilst he waits?'

'Yes, ma'am.'

'Mr Wheeler?'

'Yes, that would be fine, thank you, Major,' Kane answered. Polite without the deference of the young lad at the door. Nothing anyone would be unhappy about.

Except him.

Because now, more than ever, it was apparent to Kane that there was no future for him and Mattie. As long as they were both in green, they couldn't be together.

It would have been different if they were both commissioned officers, the way she'd pestered him to do back when they'd been little more than kids. Back then he would only have pulled her down. Now, despite fourteen years of working his way to one of the highest non-commissioned officer ranks in the British Army, the problem still remained.

He was proud of who he was, and how far he'd come. But it still wasn't good enough for Mattie, an acting colonel.

The irony wasn't lost on him.

CHAPTER SIX

MATTIE HAD NO IDEA how long she'd been avoiding returning to Kane. Or, more precisely, she knew *exactly* how long.

Not because she didn't want to go back into that room, but more because she wanted nothing *more* than to return. Her whole body felt tight, and coiled, and needy.

But giving in to temptation with Kane the other night, before they'd known about...*this*, was one thing. Now, here, it was different. She took her career seriously, and more than that she loved it, which was why she'd always taken its rules seriously. Including fraternisation.

She had never, in her entire career, had a workplace relationship—not even with a fellow commissioned officer, however brilliant any of them might have been. She'd never even been tempted. But, then, none of them had been Kane, had they?

And hadn't earlier on proved beyond all doubt that, where he was concerned, she lacked any kind of resistance whatsoever?

Which was why she'd been hiding out back here. She'd dealt with her gunshot patient's complications a good hour ago. Thankfully it hadn't been as troublesome as everyone had feared, and the young patient was now back in ICU, recovering.

And now all she could think about was how a few minutes longer in her office and she could have been naked on that desk with Kane driving into her, without a second thought for her career. A career she'd spent nearly fourteen years—ever since an officer cadet at medical school—painstakingly building up.

It was unprofessional, *reckless*, and she ought to be ashamed. Instead—and this was the worst thing about it—all she wanted to do right now was rush straight back to her office and pick up where they'd left off.

Not only had she never had a relationship with a fellow officer before, but she had also never avoided a colleague or a mission before now.

Right now, she found herself in a consultation room with a young squaddie who had come in a few days earlier complaining of a rash on his body. What had concerned her the most had been that the rash had precisely matched the shape of his body armour.

In consultation with the specialist dermatologist on her team, the two of them had agreed on a prescribed cream, but the follow-up had been set up to ensure that the rash wasn't getting worse or changing properties.

To be fair, any one of her team could have dealt with the young lad but she'd chosen to do it herself—her mind only too aware that Kane was still on the other side of the hospital, waiting for her. Which was all the proof she needed that she was putting off the inevitable.

'Okay, Fusilier, can you strip off your top half, please?'

The lad stood, peeling off his jacket and T-shirt without a trace of bashfulness. Particularly when he moved his fingers to the button of his trousers.

'You want me to take these off, too, ma'am?' he enquired casually. 'Only the rash went down there…if you remember?'

Mattie felt her lips quirk.

Oh, the confidence of youth.

'Okay, then. I'd better see.'

Peering closer, Mattie inspected the site. Interestingly, the skin was beginning to peel and the skin beneath was clear and healthy.

'And you have no other symptoms?' she checked for the third time in the last ten minutes.

'None. I feel great. And the itching has stopped.'

'All right, then, just keep applying the cream to the affected area only. Come back and see us in another two days.'

The lad began to put his clothes back on.

'So what is it?'

'We still have no idea,' she told him honestly, making her notes as she headed for the door. 'But we've taken a swab and if there's anything to tell you when the results come back, we'll call you straight in.'

'Thanks, Doc.' He grinned as she opened the consultation-room door for him, letting him out before she followed.

'No problem.' She headed for the desk, and her next patient.

'Are you still here?' Kath's voice had her swinging around, trying not to look guilty.

'Just doing a few routine consults.'

'And the liaison from Battle Group?'

So much for trying not to look guilty.

'In the mess hall, last thing I knew,' she admitted, aware that her long-term colleague was casting her a shocked look.

'Geez, Mattie, that isn't like you.'

She knew that. But it didn't really help.

'Listen, everything is under control here, and you still have that liaison to deal with, don't you? Or is there another reason you don't want to go back there?'

Mattie swung around sharply.

'Another reason?'

'Word is he's a bit of a hottie.' Kath grinned. 'One of the nurses was in the command post before you arrived the first time and took a bit of a shine to him, and the sergeant who was driving him from the Helicopter Landing Site said she wouldn't have kicked him out of bed.'

'Not exactly appropriate.' Mattie frowned, even though she felt like the biggest hypocrite around. She might have known Kath would call her out on it.

'Neither is ducking around here, trying to avoid talking to the guy. So unless you want to tell me what that's all about, I suggest you go back over there.'

With that, she pulled the list of new patients out of Mattie's hands, spun her round and guided her back down the corridor.

'Come on, I'll walk with you. I should have got off shift a couple of hours ago, as it is.'

'Fine, I'm going,' Mattie grumbled. 'How do you get all this gossip anyway?'

And more to the point, were there any whispers about her right now?

Kath laughed, unoffended.

'Because I'm a civilian doctor playing at being a reservist. You're the army doctor with rules and regulations stamped right through you like a stick of rock.'

'Right,' Mattie agreed grimly.

Except that what had happened in her office just over an hour ago had been so far removed from rules and regulations that she would have been risking her job. Or Kane his.

'Unless you're telling me you're considering breaking the rules where this guy is concerned. I also heard that he's only around his mid-thirties, which means his career has been soaring for him to get to WO2 already.'

Mattie mumbled something incoherent. She'd already

worked that out for herself, but it didn't help matters. If anything, it made them worse because it only made him more successful, and therefore that much more attractive to her.

Her main concern was that if she returned to a private room to finish ironing out the new scenarios with Kane she would find herself in yet another compromising situation with him before she could say *Case simulation zero one.* Again.

Worse, some insubordinate side of her *wanted* it to happen again.

They were at the mess doors before Mattie could find another excuse. And then, like a parent waiting to watch their kid go into school on the first day, Kath gave her a gentle push and waited at the doors until she stepped inside.

She saw Kane immediately.

'You're still in here?' She would never know how she made her objecting feet cross the room towards him and fold themselves over the bench so she sat on the opposite side of the table from him in an otherwise empty mess hall.

In a couple of hours it would be heaving again. Just not now.

'Where else was I to go?' he enquired smoothly, before lowering his voice so it was just loud enough for her to hear. 'Besides, after…before, I thought it might be advisable to continue the discussion in a more public setting.'

No one could overhear them where they were, but they could be seen. Privacy to talk, without the temptation to touch. It made complete sense, so why did she feel so suddenly deflated? Mattie forced a bright smile.

'Yes. Right. Good idea.'

He eyed her darkly but said nothing. There was no need to feel this urge to fill the silence.

'We have less than twenty-four hours to get through. Then you'll be back at Battle Group.'

And this time she wouldn't harbour any foolish notions that they could pick up where they'd left off that night in the hotel. She had to put it out of her mind. Just like she had fourteen years ago.

Because back then it worked out so well, a little voice needled in her head, but Mattie resolutely ignored it, although it made her stomach hurt.

'Why didn't you tell me that you'd joined up?' she asked. 'More than that, that the army has been your career for the past decade and a half?'

'I didn't think it mattered.'

'You're a CSM, Kane.' She shook her head. 'To make that rank in such a short time means you must have been flying from practically the moment you went on your recruits course. People are in for eighteen, or twenty years and they don't even make it half as far.'

'I got some lucky breaks.'

'It's more than that,' she snorted. 'You've dedicated your life to it. And you always dismissed the military. You hated my father being a brigadier, and you slated my dream of being a doctor in the army.'

'I was an arrogant kid who thought he knew it all.' Kane barked a humourless laugh. 'An idiot.'

'So what changed?'

He sucked in a breath, his wide chest expanding even further.

'*I* did, Mattie.'

'You?'

'People can, you know.'

Of course she knew that. But it hardly clarified anything for her. Everything was still as murky and confusing as ever.

'I always thought my father paid you to leave.'

He pulled his lips into a thin line, but it took a while for him to answer.

'I always wondered what he'd told you,' he remarked evenly.

It didn't answer her question.

'He didn't tell me that. I just thought maybe he had, and that's why you hadn't said goodbye.' Still, he didn't answer. She tried again. 'What I mean is, *did* he pay you to leave?'

The distant clatter of the cooks across the mess hall stopped the silence from being too oppressive. Still Kane didn't answer, and Mattie wondered if she was about to go insane with the need to know.

'Did he pay you, Kane?' she pressed at last.

Kane eyed her for a moment longer.

'What *did* he tell you?'

'Nothing.' She blew out heavily in exasperation, thrusting aside the stab of grief that sliced through her. 'Although maybe that's because he started suffering from Alzheimer's six years ago. Or at least that's what we think, in hindsight. He's been getting progressively worse these last three years, though.'

'Oh, hell. I'm so sorry, Matz.' A genuinely sad expression clouded Kane's face. 'I hope you never blamed him for me leaving.'

If she hadn't have known how Kane and her father had rubbed each other up the wrong way, she might have actually thought it was more than just sympathy on Kane's part. That he was saddened on a more personal level.

She waggled her head from side to side, trying to shake off the melancholy.

'I didn't. I blamed you,' she told him simply. 'For leaving. And for taking the money, if there was any.'

'I'm glad.'

And she didn't doubt that Kane was sincere. She offered a wry smile.

'However much my father and I might have clashed when I was going through my rebellious teens, I always knew he had my back. He always loved me.'

'If it hadn't been for you, and Hayden, and your parents, I would never have known what a true, loving family could look like,' Kane said quietly, a moment of unguarded wistfulness.

Mattie thought her chest would crack open with the effort to contain itself. She stamped it down quickly.

'So, did he pay you, Kane?'

Another beat, and then...

'No.'

She wasn't expecting the numbness that crept over her so abruptly. Her throat suddenly tight. The answer she'd wanted to hear but hadn't really believed she would.

'He didn't?' she whispered.

'He did not,' Kane confirmed. 'What's more, if he had tried, I wouldn't have accepted it. No amount of money could have made me walk away from you.'

It was as if some giant concrete block had been sitting on her chest and she hadn't even realised it. But now it had lifted. Gone. Something was swelling inside her chest and she didn't care to evaluate that too closely, but either way she could breathe again.

'You *did* walk away from me, though,' she managed instead. 'So, if not for money...then *why*?'

'For your own good, Mattie.' His face shuttered instantly. Effectively locking her out.

Strangely, instead of making her back off, it sent a sliver of anger through her.

'What kind of answer is that?'

'The only one you're going to get.'

Her heart started thumping slowly in her chest.

'Well, that isn't good enough, Kane.'

'That's too bad.'

'It's been fourteen years.' She blew out a breath. 'And you still can't tell me? What can possibly matter that much?'

'Because it's my story, Mattie. My past. I don't want it all raked up now and, what's more, I don't believe it will achieve anything to do so.'

'It's *our* past,' she corrected furiously, reining herself in sharply as she cast a glance at the kitchen area.

But no one was watching. As far as they were concerned it was two senior ranking soldiers discussing a brigade issue. They couldn't know what the topic really was.

'I think I deserve that much.'

He snagged her eyes with his. Searching them. Making her feel utterly naked.

'What would be the point, Mattie?' he demanded hoarsely. Quietly. 'Two days ago, maybe I would have. When I thought that maybe things could be different between us the next time.'

'You mean when you thought I'd left the army?' she asked dully. 'Before I even knew you'd ever joined up?'

'Yes. Back *then*,' he confirmed.

'So you'd thought that maybe we could have a future? You really had intended to search me out the moment you returned from this exercise?'

'Why else do you think I gave you my number?'

'And would you have told me then? Would you have said that you were one of the most senior NCOs in the British Army?'

'I would have.' He dipped his head slowly. Once. 'But we both know that it's impossible now.'

How was it possible for hope to flourish in one part of her chest, only for it to be extinguished in another?

'Unless one of us leaves,' she posited carefully.

He studied her, his expression guarded.

'And have you any plans to do that?'

She stared at him. He couldn't be serious.

'You were going to once before,' he reminded her, seeming to read her thoughts. 'When you were marrying your Earl Blakeney.'

'True, but it would have been a mistake, I realise that now.' She shook her head sadly. 'I never wanted to leave— it was just what was expected of me.'

And she'd been trying to convince herself that she'd moved on. From Kane. Not that she was about to admit that now.

'I would have ended up resenting him for it sooner or later. And the marriage would have failed.'

'So you're saying that seeing me—or thinking you imagined me—at your wedding rehearsal saved you from making a mistake that would have hurt both of you?'

She couldn't be sure whether he understood too little or too much. Either way, she wasn't sure she wanted to go down that route.

'Remember that promotion I mentioned I was getting?' she asked, changing tack swiftly. The one he must have imagined was in a civilian capacity. 'Well, it's to half-colonel, back at Brigade.'

There was a beat.

'Congratulations.'

His voice was to level. Too even. As though he was picking his words too carefully. Guarding himself from the inevitable.

The way that she should be.

Instead, a complicated knot of emotions was moving inside her. Surging back and forth, even as her heart was numb.

'What about you? You're Company Sergeant Major. What's next for you? I heard that you've been inundated with offers to join the private sector.'

'Where did you hear that?' he scoffed.

'Kane, the instant you walked into my field hospital looking like…that…' she waved her hand to encompass him '…all the single female soldiers took notice. The rumour mill went into overdrive.'

'I'm flattered.'

'Oh, come on, you know as well as I do that half the girls fancied you when we were back in Heathdale. Even your family name didn't put them off.'

'Only half?' he teased, but it was a careful teasing, like he was really just changing the subject.

They both knew it.

'The point is, you could change career if you wanted. Leave the army and go into the private sector. There's a lot more money in that.'

'Of all people, I'd expect you to know this isn't about money, Mattie,' he chastised her gently, and heat raced to her cheeks.

He was right, she *did* know that. It had always been about being part of something special. More than just a family. Something that was bigger than her. Something that mattered.

She bobbed her head but didn't answer.

'We don't have a future, Mattie.'

He left the statement hanging, giving her a chance to refute it the way she wanted to. *Oh, how she wanted to.* But she couldn't. He was right, they didn't have a future.

She could feel emotion welling up inside her, threatening to effervesce and spill out everywhere. But, as Kane had said himself, what good would it do to give in to it? To let it out?

With a superhuman effort she pulled herself together, fighting through the threatening tears—and she never cried—to focus on the paperwork on the table in front of her.

'Okay,' she began, swallowing back a lump of…something

in her throat. 'So, the purpose of the medical simulations we run on these occasions won't be to train my medical team. We've run all the scenarios multiple times and the teams all know exactly what they're doing. The aim is to stress the new tactical brigade. To test them, and to find any weaknesses.'

She wouldn't have objected if Kane had taken the conversation back to the personal. But he didn't. As she'd known he wouldn't.

'Yes.' He offered her a half-smile. His only acknowledgement that they were trying to move past everything. 'You can benefit, of course. But initially the scenarios will test the individual soldier out there on the front line. It will test the company. But most of all for Operation Strikethrough, these initial scenarios have been designed to test and stress the new strike battalion's medical chain and handovers.'

'So we'll start with relatively standard scenarios and cas-evacs.'

'Some cas-evacs on the bonnets of four-by-fours to an FOB,' Kane agreed, indicting the Forward Operating Base and making notes accordingly, as she tried not to let her gaze linger on that hand that had touched her, held her, the way that no one else had ever quite managed before or since.

'And if that runs smoothly and the chain holds out, we'll also look to delay medical support for…shall we say forty minutes initially,' confirmed Mattie, as though she didn't feel broken. Exposed. As if she would never quite be right again.

'Keeping the patient alive and stable enough for transport. Consider nutrition, hydration, et cetera whilst the recovery vehicle finds a way in.'

'Right, so, like I said, we may need to find a new grid reference if things keep advancing the way they have been.

It's going to be our job to fly out and assess the site together, as well as assess the guys during the scenario itself.'

'I know.' She tried to tell herself that it was no big deal. She was a professional with over a decade of experience. She'd never let herself get into a compromising situation before. But, then, Kane had never been involved before.

At least they would be able to work through the assessment and feedback separately, feeding the findings up through the chain of command and letting them iron any issues out at Brigade level.

'Can you handle this, Mattie?' he asked, and she tried not to notice that he hadn't called her *Matz* in the entire time he'd been at the field hospital.

She suspected that, if it had not felt completely insane, he probably would have addressed her as *ma'am* as a way to keep that line of separation all the clearer.

He'd have to address her more formally if anyone else were to overhear their conversation. It worried her that she didn't know if she'd prefer that or not. He seemed to be finding this—resisting each other—far easier than she was.

Except that he was the one who had reached for her back in her office.

The thought left a warm glow as it wound slowly through her.

'Can you handle working together this closely?' he added, as though he thought she needed clarification.

'Of course I can handle it,' she bristled, despite the fact that she'd only just been asking herself the same question. But, then, he'd always known just how to push her buttons. 'The question is, Kane, *can you*?'

CHAPTER SEVEN

MATTIE SKIMMED THE notes of her fourth patient so far, before heading into the consultation room. Theoretically, as CO she had plenty of things to do other than routine examinations, but she'd always liked to keep her hand in, carrying out the occasional check-up to see what was going on at ground level in her hospital.

Besides, although the hospital was so often in a flurry of activity, there were sometimes a few days of downtime, especially just before or after a big exercise. And right now, doing an occasional consultation kept her mind from wandering to Kane.

She felt better this morning, although she didn't know why since she'd spent most of the night tossing and turning, pretending that she wasn't thinking about Kane, or imagining him on his own cot bed a few army tents over. By zero four hundred hours she'd given up trying to sleep and had dressed and slipped into her office to catch up on some admin, ploughing through a decent amount of work. Nonetheless, a corner of her mind had been distracted, thoughts of Kane weaving around her head.

By now he would be with Kath, her second in command, observing the medical scenarios she had set up for her own teams to keep them sharp and focused. It was part of his job as liaison, and it provided them with a chance for him to see what her unit practised, which could then be dovetailed into the scenarios they would work up for the infantry medics.

Mattie had almost been tempted to head down there and see him—see what he made of it, she corrected hastily. If wouldn't have been that unusual for the CO to attend, especially with the place enjoying this brief lull. But, in the end, she'd chosen instead to come to the walk-in clinic and spend a half-hour or so seeing what kind of cases were walking in at the moment.

Like this private who was apparently suffering from back pain. Satisfied with the notes, she went into the consultation room, smiling at the young lad sitting side-on on the examination bed. He looked as though being in the field hospital was the last place he wanted to be, but was in too much discomfort to avoid making the visit any longer.

'Hello, Private, what brings you in today?'

'Yeah… Hey, ma'am… I guess… I guess I've got a bit of a sore back.' He pulled a face.

'Upper or lower?'

'Um…around here…' He reached round carefully to indicate.

'Is the pain new?' Mattie asked.

The lad shook his head.

'It's been hurting me for a while now, maybe eight months on and off, but it's getting pretty bad now, and the pain has started shooting down my leg.'

'Right.' Mattie nodded. 'Done anything particularly strenuous recently?'

Again the young private shook his head.

'I'm always in the gym, working out, you know? Some weights, and lots of PT. Nothing unusual.'

'Jumping out of planes?'

'Yeah. Sure.'

'Okay, let's give you a physical. Check your reflexes,

muscle strength and stuff. Which leg is experiencing the shooting pain?'

'Left.' He tapped his thigh.

'Okay, let's start with your right leg. Lift it up, bending your knee so that's against your chest, and try to resist as I push down. Good. Okay, try the left leg. Good.'

For the next few minutes Mattie went through a series of tests, chatting to him as she went and eliciting more information. Ultimately, everything seemed to confirm her original suspicion that he had a herniated disc.

'Okay,' Her test complete, she sat back on the chair opposite to chat to him. 'So, I suspect you have a bit of bulging in one of the discs between your vertebrae. It can press on the nerve and cause some of the pain you've described for me.'

'That goes away by itself, right?' the lad asked hopefully.

Mattie smiled. They were all the same, soldiers.

'It should do,' she told him. 'But only if you take care of it. That means getting you on the timetable with the physical therapist for some rehab, and accepting you'll have some limitations on what you can do whilst it heals.'

'So I'm out of training?' He pulled a face. 'It isn't that bad really, ma'am.'

'If you want to heal fast, then you'll listen,' Mattie told him firmly, knowing how these guys could feel pressure to get back to their units before they'd given their bodies chance to fully heal. 'I'll be passing it along the chain of command so that your CO knows you need time to heal, but ultimately the more you take care of it now, the faster you will actually be able to get back out there.

'Do I need an X-ray to confirm it?' He pulled another face.

Mattie smiled. 'No, don't worry. An X-ray won't detect a herniated disc. It might just rule out other causes, but at this stage I don't have any reason to suspect anything else.'

He blew out heavily.

'How long, then?'

'Piece of string,' she told him, not unkindly. 'Come on, let's get you out of here and into the physical therapy unit. With any luck they might even have a slot this morning.'

As she walked the private out and tasked one of the nurses with getting him an appointment with the physio, she turned back for her next patient's notes, only to find Kane standing there.

'Mr Wheeler.' She plastered a friendly smile on her lips, aware that there were plenty of ears around right at that moment.

'Major Brigham,' he acknowledged.

'I trust you had an informative morning with Major Donal. I know she ran through some of the scenarios we've been practising here, so that you see how we can dovetail with medical situations for your guys.'

'Yes, I have some thoughts on how we can integrate it. When you're available, I'd like to go back to the map and run you through where our different units are going to be, and when.'

'Of course.' Mattie nodded. After all, dealing with this mission for Battle group was the priority. 'Give me a moment.'

Reaching for the patient list, she made a couple of notes, nodded to the nurse, and gestured for Kane to join her.

'Shall we, Mr Wheeler?'

And her pulse wasn't really leaping in her throat at the idea of being alone again with Kane—away from all her sharp-eyed staff.

They might not have clocked anything yet but one wrong move, one misplaced word and they would instantly know something was amiss.

'I saw one of the scenarios you were looking at was apparently a splenic injury,' he remarked as they began their walk down the corridor past other colleagues.

'Yes, blunt splenic injuries were always notoriously challenging to manage when on deployment, not only because field posts may not have angiographic capabilities to confirm hemoperitoneum, in which case the casualty would need immediate evacuation for surgical treatment, but also because NOM of splenic injuries could put the casualty at risk of prolonged hypotension.'

'NOM?'

'Sorry, Non-operative management.'

'Right.'

'The other question concerns whether the need for immediate splenectomy can differ between those splenic injures in a patient also suffering from severe brain injury and those patients with splenic injury with no severe brain injury.'

Reaching her office door, she opened it and invited Kane inside, before hesitating for a moment then propping it open slightly. When she turned, he was watching her, those deep cocoa pools drawing her in, leaving her breathless. She stopped, almost daring him to comment. But he said nothing, simply waiting for her to round her desk and take her seat before sitting down himself.

'I think we should start over. Yesterday was a bit of a...' She searched for the word, her normally sharp brain obviously still a little dented.

'Shock,' he supplied wryly.

'Shock,' she echoed.

'I think that's a wise idea,' he began seriously, before his lips twitched upwards. 'Hello, Major Brigham, I'm WO2 Wheeler.'

'Not that far back,' she objected, but he'd made her laugh and she felt a little of her awkwardness dissipate. 'Though I still can't believe you're an army guy.'

'No, I understand that.' He shrugged, and she appreciated that he still wasn't going to be drawn on his reasons.

It made her feel oddly shut out. He'd never shut her out
once during their entire relationship all those years ago.
Well, apart from the very end, of course, so that probably
wasn't the best comparison to make.

Hurt lanced through her, cold and steel-like, and she
tried to grab hold of it as though she thought she might
somehow wrap it around her chest and protect herself. She
told herself that as much as she longed to know his reasons,
it was going to be better to leave well alone.

Far better to hold onto the knowledge that they had a
job to do, and that people's lives in the future could hinge
on how well she and Kane could pull things together now.
And, despite everything else, she prided herself on being
a good OC. Clearly Kane was a good WO2.

So, for now, that would he enough.

'Fine.' She made herself pick up her brief. 'Then let's
run through the original exercise plans. Our main phase
is running medical simulations with the battle group to
test the support chain. This pre-phase now is about running our own medical scenarios to keep us sharp in a
medical sense.'

'Right, so your main phase is obviously just a medical phase in our battle group's schedule. Brigade are now
looking to break that element down further so that we have
two distinct medical support chain phases.'

'Run me through it.' Clicking her pen, Mattie began
making notes.

'Initially we'd be running the scenarios in the briefing.'

'Which means individual or small group scenarios.'
Mattie nodded, not needing to check her notes but doing
so anyway. To keep her fingers busy, if nothing else. 'To
check how the support chain holds up with the new tactics.'

'Right. Then, depending how that goes, we'll tweak the

tactics or support logistics and keep running those scenarios until we know they're smooth.'

It was almost odd, seeing Kane flip so suddenly. A side of him that had always been there but which she'd never pictured in this military setting before—probably because he'd been so anti-establishment. Yet seeing him now, it was easy to see why he was already a WO2.

'Agreed,' she clipped out, pulling her head back to where it should be.

'But Brigade also want to see if we can look at how a mass casualty incident could be approached.'

'For this exercise?' She cocked her head at him, her mind already beginning to build up a possible event.

'Not necessarily. But possibly. You know how Brigade works.'

'Hurry up and wait.' She nodded. 'Yes. I know. So they want us to start drawing something up in case, but otherwise it can shelved for a future battle group exercise?'

'Pretty much.'

And Mattie couldn't say what happened, or how, but like a switch flicking on they were suddenly in a different place. Talking and tabling suggestions as though they were any OC and WO2. Not Mattie and Kane.

Their intimate history was no longer an issue. If anything, Mattie was shocked to find it made the process even easier, because they knew each other so well they could pre-empt what the other was thinking or read the other's body language.

And when that part of the discussion drew to a natural pause, it was startling to realise they'd been talking for almost ninety minutes. Yet when she stood up to stretch her legs, intending to move around the room, she found herself naturally drifting towards Kane.

'For the record,' she heard herself say quietly, 'I think

now that we're over the initial…shock of meeting out here, we will be able to work well together.'

He regarded her for a moment, his expression turning sober. Though she wished she could read exactly what was behind that slightly guarded expression.

'I really think we can, Mattie. The army is in your blood, it's who you are and you're very good at it, anyone can see that. And I know you don't understand how I came to be here, but I can tell you that the army saved me. I'm not here because my CO needed someone to fill a gap, I'm here because I'm good at what I do.'

'Obviously.' She eyed him with surprise. 'Did you think I didn't realise that? You wouldn't have made it to CSM if you weren't, and certainly not in under a decade and a half. You have to be exceptional at what you do.'

'Not bad for a Wheeler kid, eh?' He laughed self-deprecatingly.

Mattie didn't laugh with him.

'You were never like them, Kane,' she said after a moment. 'You always had the capability to make something of yourself. I just think… I just think that too many people around Heathdale were small–minded, saying that you'd never amount to anything, and you believed them. But I never thought that.'

He watched her again, those rich, brown pools swirling like a vortex. They would drag her under if she let them.

'No,' he said quietly. 'You never did, did you? You always believed in me.'

She bobbed her head in the fraught silence, not trusting herself to answer past the painful lump in her throat.

'I never wanted to let you down, Matz.' His harsh voice sliced unexpectedly through the air.

'Why did you leave?'

He looked simultaneously angry and sad.

'I had to.'

'Without a word of explanation? Without saying goodbye?'

'You think leaving was me letting you down.' He exhaled heavily, his fist thumping heavily on his lap. 'But that isn't what I meant. I let you down before that. Leaving was the solution, not the problem.'

'There you go, talking in riddles again,' she said quietly. 'But you never actually tell me anything.'

'I can't tell you,' he growled, his eyes glittering with fury.

But not at her, she realised. At himself. At his past.

'Can't?' She dropped her voice again, not wanting to attract any attention from out in the corridor. 'Or won't?'

He studied her, as if the words were taking their time to permeate his brain. As if he was really evaluating them. And then, for the second time in two days, he swept the proverbial rug out from beneath her.

'I did something…' He lifted his hand. 'Before we started dating. Before we even met. I was fifteen, but I committed a crime.'

'*You* did?' Mattie sat up straighter in her seat.

She knew what his father was like. What his brothers were like. But not Kane. Still, he'd been fifteen, it surely couldn't have been that serious.

'It's something I'm ashamed of, even to this day. But that night—the very night I told you I loved you—what I'd done years before caught up with me. That's why I left.'

'You ran away?' She was confused.

'No,' he answered instantly. Vehemently. 'I did not run away.'

'But you left?'

'I faced up to it, Mattie. I took responsibility. In doing so I was offered a way out that I hadn't been expecting.'

The army, she realised abruptly. Plenty of lads joined the military because it was that or juvie. Or crime. Some ended up bringing their problems with them, but many of them went on to become incredible soldiers. She'd just never considered Kane would be one of them.

He must really have been some soldier to get past that start to where he was now. Yet she could well believe it.

But that meant that he had even more to lose than she did if either of them crossed that line again. All the more reason for them snuff out this chemistry that they shared and concentrate on the task at hand, hammering out the smoothest, most successful operation phase that they could.

'Then you deserve everything you've earned,' she said sincerely. 'I'm full of admiration. And I'm even impressed with your CO. I thought Percy Copperhead was a snob who would have been hung up on things like that. I thought he'd sent you here to try to undermine me.'

She probably shouldn't have admitted it. She wouldn't have admitted it to anyone else. But, then, she wouldn't have been in this position with anyone other than Kane. Besides, he'd finally shared a confidence with her, and it felt like they'd turned a corner. Being open with him could surely only help them to get things back on track.

'Oh, no, the guy's a first-class oxygen thief.' Kane laughed abruptly. 'If it was down to him, I'd be thrown out of the army even now. As would half the lads in the company, even though a raft of them were true heroes in multiple tours over the last ten years. But Copperhead only took over as CO a couple of months ago, it was my old CO who championed his guys.'

Why didn't that surprise her?

'So sending you here…?'

'Gets me out of his face. He likes yes-men around him, and I'm not one of those.'

'No,' Mattie snorted. 'You're not. So, if we really want to hack the guy off then we just need to make this the most enviable phase of the exercise.'

'Couldn't hurt,' Kane agreed.

'No more...*this*...' She waved her hands between them, hoping Kane understood all the words she couldn't bring herself to say aloud.

Chemistry. Passion. Lust.

She refused to acknowledge any other L-word because that, obviously, wasn't applicable here.

'It's still going to be there, Matz,' Kane answered in a low, only half-regretful tone that spiralled heat straight through her to pool right between her legs. 'We just have to move past it.'

'Ignore it,' she suggested.

'Use it to our advantage.' He shrugged. 'We understand each other in a way no one else will understand. Anticipate each other.'

'Even now, over a decade later?'

She already knew the answer, yet some perverse part of her wanted to hear him say it.

'If you have to ask the question then think back to last weekend in that hotel room,' he growled deliciously, 'and then decide how well I know you.'

It was thrilling. Exhilarating. And entirely the opposite of what they were trying to achieve.

'This isn't exactly *moving past it*.' She arched her eyebrows at him, even as she bit her tongue to stop herself from flicking it out to moisten her dry lips.

He countered her with a look that was so sensual she wanted to walk round the desk and straddle him, there and then.

'Then start trying,' he told her.

'Fine.' She didn't need to tell him that it seemed the more they tried, the harder it became. 'Tomorrow morning we're running a medical scenario on a MERT if you want to come. I'm sure you've observed before but might help give you an idea of what goes on when your guys hand over the injured soldier to us. We'll be running two casualties from the same scenario with very similar injuries.'

'What is the benefit of that?' he asked curiously.

'The casualty who is slightly more severely wounded will receive textbook treatment on the ground before our MERT team arrives, whilst the casualty who's slightly less severely wounded will have mistakes made by the combat medics.'

'Okay.' Kane nodded. 'So that way, when we run the simulations in my setting for my men, your teams will already be prepared for any less than optimal treatment on the ground?'

'That way we can be sure the test is on your men rather than my medics. Which is the goal of this new phase.'

'Call it a pre-phase.' Mattie offered a smile. 'The original first phase, which is the one we'd already planned, is geared around testing the medical support chain for the battle group rather than the medical knowledge of either your guys or my medical staff.'

'Which it is still intended to be, it's just a matter of whether we need to find new grid locations. And the pre-planned second phase, which should also be changed, is going to be a full mass casualty event, same grid locations as those already planned with the Engineers.'

CHAPTER EIGHT

HE HADN'T INTENDED to join her, yet Kane found himself falling in step as they ran over the rough terrain together.

He'd been following her for four miles so far, ever since his alarm had gone off half an hour earlier and he'd decided to see if a run would clear his head. At first he'd thought it better to stay back, off Mattie's radar. But following that delectable body, clad in tight running gear that moulded itself to every delicious curve, had definitely not been helping to keep his libido in check.

At least running alongside her meant he couldn't stay just the right distance behind her, ogling her like some kind of hyped-up teenage boy. It'd been altogether too tempting to pull her into the nearby treeline and take her up against one of those silver birches. All he could think of was the way her long legs had appeared even longer, reminding him of the way she'd wrapped them around his hips that night at the hotel. Locking them over his back and using them to pull him deeper and deeper inside her.

God, he was losing it again.

Concentrating on his running, Kane willed his body back into submission. No easy feat when her ragged breathing was now causing a slightly different memory. The damned woman was enough to drive him insane.

And he wasn't even sure she knew it.

Mattie swung her head round, saw him running beside her and slowly—reluctantly, he thought—pulled her earphones out of her ears.

'I thought you'd be in the gym.'

'I've always preferred running.' He shrugged, then frowned. 'Why?'

'I don't know…the muscles.'

She flushed as she said it, the tell she'd been trying to hide. The giveaway that she'd paid him more attention than she wanted to admit to—thinking of him the way he'd been thinking of her. Kane barely supressed a grin.

'That's just genuine physical work,' he told her. 'No hours of weights in the gym.'

At least out here they were safe. Safe to talk in privacy, but also safe that it wasn't intimate. Nothing could happen.

'If the offer is still on the table for the MERT ride-along, I'd like to see that.'

'What changed your mind?'

He couldn't tell whether she was hacked off or happy about it and, for some reason, that got under his skin.

'I figured it could only help me to know what to focus on for my guys if I saw for myself how their packaging of the casualties affects your team.'

It was a valid reason, and one he certainly *should* have in the forefront of his mind. If was just a shame that the main reason started with *Spending more time* and ended on *with Mattie*.

Even the thought of her was helping to elevate his temperature, and as much as he'd like to blame it on the run, he couldn't. With an irritated grumble, Kane hauled off his running tee and tucked it into the rear waistband of his shorts.

'Do you really need to take that off?'

'Sorry?' He turned to look at her, assuming that this was her idea of a joke, getting him back for earlier.

Instead, he realised that her expression was deadly serious, and slightly anguished.

She wanted him, too.

'I do,' he replied with nonchalance.

If she wanted his chest covered, she could always order him to do it. He'd spent years thinking he'd lost her and missing her in a way he'd never dreamed possible. Now it was Mattie's turn to wonder at things that might have been.

The fact that she didn't told him everything he needed to know. Instead, they ran in quiet companionship together. Their step and their breathing reaching an easy harmony.

'It's so quiet,' he observed after a while.

'Peaceful,' agreed Mattie. 'And beautiful. Like those flowers over there. Whatever they are.'

He followed the direction of her gaze.

'Lupins.'

'Sorry?'

'The flowers. They're lupins.'

He couldn't help smiling as her head swivelled around, knowing what she was about to say even before she said it.

'I read it.'

'You read it?'

'In a book about this place,' he continued, with deliberate nonchalance. 'I like to do that when I go somewhere new. It's good to learn new things.'

An echo of something she'd once said to him as kids, he wondered if she remembered it.

'Yes,' she managed quietly, telling him that she did remember. 'I know.'

'Some things don't change, Matz.'

She looked at him and paused before answering.

'And some things do. It isn't always easy to see which it is. Or if it's for the best.'

'Sometimes it's better to just let your gut tell you.'

'So, what does your gut tell you, Kane?'

He shrugged, not answering for a moment. Another time he might have offered a dismissive quip. This time he didn't want to.

'I don't know,' he admitted at last. 'That's why I'm out here, running. Trying to clear my head.'

She eyed him again, but this time her gaze was softer. He thought it might be his undoing.

'I thought you were going to just say, *My gut's telling me I'm hungry.* Or some other clever remark.'

'I considered it,' he answered wryly. 'I opted against clever remarks, for the truth.'

She bobbed her head but didn't answer. They were all alone out here, no one was round. No one could even see them. For a moment he wanted to just grab her, kiss her and tell her everything was going to be okay.

But it wasn't. Because nothing had changed.

Except for the fact that he could no longer pretend he was over her.

'We get such odd periods through a day in this place.' Her soft voice broke through his thoughts. He realised she was trying to keep the topic light. Or, at least, not intimate. He welcomed it. 'Sometimes there's so much downtime you think you're going crazy, and other times it's so completely full on that you think you must already have *gone* crazy.

'That's life in the army.' He forced a laugh. 'I remember your father always used to say it, too. I'm so sorry about the Alzheimer's.'

And about the fact that she didn't know that it had been her father who had helped him to get into the army in the first instance. Yet she couldn't know. He'd already told her as much as he dared, and if there was a little shame involved on his part, well, that was his issue to deal with.

It was bad enough that he'd had to drag her father into his family's problems back then. He hated that pretty much thirty-five years on this earth still hadn't been long enough for him to work out a way to finally get away from the destructive impact his shameful family had on anyone around them.

Including himself.

Although the worst of it was that his actions that night had been of his own making. If he'd just called the police...

Even now he could hear it all. The shouts. The shots. The way the tyres had screeched in the night.

It was only when he felt a hand grabbing at his arm that he realised he'd been accelerating harder and harder, and now he could feel his breath ragged and painful in his chest.

It was almost welcome.

'Slow down,' Mattie grumbled. 'It's a training run, not a race.'

Abruptly, he slowed then stopped, fighting to regain his breathing as she bent over, her hands braced against her knees, her words choppy.

'What was all that about?'

'Sorry,' he managed curtly, steeling himself.

He didn't want all his doubts and regrets to be plastered all over his face when she eventually looked up again.

'I'm going back,' he barked. 'Get a shower before I go on that MERT shout later.'

'Kane...'

But he didn't wait. He couldn't afford to. They were a good few miles out from the hospital accommodation and, out here alone with Mattie, he feared he might be prepared to tell her anything.

Everything.

But he couldn't. Because right now she already knew that he had betrayed her. She didn't need to know he'd dragged her father—and ultimately Hayden—into the lie, too. So, instead, Kane concentrated on the run. The pounding impact of his body racing over the harsh terrain.

Cracking out a crushing pace was just what he needed to get his head back in order.

'Everyone has their job, don't they?' Kane yelled as the helicopter landed near the simulated blast site.

Mattie duly glanced at each member of the Medical Emergency Response Team.

She'd made a conscious decision to put the morning's odd run behind them. She wanted to pretend it was for the good of the exercise—and there was certainly an element of that to it—but deep down there was also the fear that if she pressed Kane on whatever this morning had been about, he would only back off from her all the more.

And it was pointless trying to tell herself that she didn't care. Clearly, she did.

Even though she shouldn't.

So, instead, she focused on his question, and the task in hand.

'Yeah, everyone knows their role. One of the paramedics will be charged with tourniquets, field dressings, logroll. The nurse will be monitoring, so we know pulse rates, saturations, rhythms. Could be radial, femoral or carotid depending on degree of sickness.

'The doctor will be doing the ABCs, and the second paramedic will be putting in cannulas for fluids or bloods. So, yeah, everyone has their designated jobs.'

This time it might be a simulation scenario, but it was all too familiar to her. Over the last decade she had done this for real on multiple tours of duty, just as the four medics she was assessing today had done. However, she'd never worked with any of them before, which made today's simulation all the more important.

And the fact that Kane was on board, so very close to

her, only complicated things that little bit more. Not that she couldn't handle the pressure, of course. More that it was incredibly draining having her body on full alert almost every minute of the day. Attuned to his presence whether she wanted to be or not.

Surely this mini-exercise would be something she could get stuck into, and it would help her to clear Kane from her thoughts, even a little while.

'Okay, Sergeant Cole,' she shouted above the roar of the rotor blades, 'I'm designating you as the liaison for this shout. I'll be accompanying you on the ground but I'm there to observe only, so just continue as though you were alone.'

The sergeant confirmed her understanding, then they both covered their mouths as the helicopter descended, raising huge swathes of dusty air in its wake.

She'd be looking to see how well the sergeant liaised with the medics on the ground. The simulation was a bomb blast near the FIBUA, so Mattie was also keen to see how the medics on the ground had carried out their own medical procedures.

'I don't need to remind you that the point of the MERT crew is to essentially move the field hospital to the patient. As the doctor and medical staff on board you have the knowledge to treat, anaesthetise, even operate on the patient in-flight.'

She glanced around the group, hoping all of them could hear her—or at least read her lips—over the noise of the engines.

'But for the MERT crew to do a good job, the soldiers on site must have done their basics properly, which means applying combat application tourniquets in good time and tying them off tightly, getting the field dressings on, administering morphine, and ensuring they are ready with really accurate MIST handovers. That means we they need to have really identified the Mechansim of Injury, the Injury pattern, the Signs or observations, and the Treatment given. And that's what today is all about. Not us saving this guy, but us seeing if the lads out there, in the thick of the fighting, have done the best job they can do for their buddies, under the most intense circumstances.'

As the helicopter landed, Mattie followed the sergeant off so that she could continue assessing. Kane was only feet away.

'Okay, what have we got?'

'Patient one is a double amputee, mechanism of injury IED. Due to the loss of limbs there was no radial pulse, so we put a sternal IO into his chest to push fluids through.'

Which would have meant manually forcing the fluids through the injured soldier's sternum, an incredible painful procedure. Mattie continued to assess.

'Patient two was hit by an IED whilst travelling in a vehicle. The vehicle overturned and impaled him on some rebar. Although the rebar has been left in place, it was too long and had to be cut down. A field dressing was used to staunch the bleeding.

'Patient three has a gunshot wound to his chest. Entry wound but no exit wound. The wound has been cleaned and packed. He had no radial pulse and minimal external bleeding. Needle compression resulted in return of radial as well as easier breathing.'

Satisfied, the sergeant directed the lads to ferry the three casualties to the waiting helicopter, where the MERT team would be ready.

CHAPTER NINE

THE LULL OF the four-by-four had been almost soothing as they'd begun their recce the following day. A corporal was acting as their designated driver, and she and Kane had been in the back, sitting opposite each other on the hard metal seats that lined each side, ostensibly poring over the map and the potential sites. Going through the scenarios one more time to determine what kind of cas-evac would be ideal for each. Helicopter? Vehicle? Ambulance?

But a couple of hours in and the tension that had begun winding between them ever since they'd set off had become fraught, and thick.

It had started with the first sway of the vehicle as Mattie's leg had rocked against Kane's. She'd moved it away, trying to create some space, but as they'd moved from the level tracks around the hospital onto the more uneven ground of the landscape the rocking motion had grown more pronounced.

With every passing minute, and each brush of her leg against his, each moment of delicious friction, Mattie had felt her resolve slipping. She'd tried to focus on different things in the space. The jerry cans, the sticker, the stretcher behind Kane's head. Yet nothing had worked and, instead, all the professional attitude they'd been focused on had crumbled with each roll of the cab. Especially when Kane had snagged her gaze with his and slowly, slowly moved his thigh—hard and defined—to pin hers in place. As though his resolve was as fragile as hers.

As though he'd *wanted* as badly as she did.

There was no way that the corporal driving the vehicle would possibly have detected anything, and yet Mattie had felt instantly exposed. Edgy. Like they'd been teenagers caught necking in the back of a taxi. Except that it wasn't a taxi, they weren't teenagers, and they sure as hell hadn't been necking.

But she'd wanted to.

She *still* wanted to.

And now, several tense hours later, the four-by-four having left the main track for off-road terrain, and the wallowing becoming more and more pronounced, the contact was becoming almost unbearable.

'Bit rough, isn't it?' Kane murmured, pitched low enough for their driver not to hear in the front.

She blinked slowly, the tone sounding innocent enough but the glint in his eyes suggesting anything but. Despite everything they'd said the other day in her office, a wicked thrill poured through her in an instant.

She didn't mean to, but Mattie felt her eyes drop to his mouth. She'd avoided looking at him for the last few days but now that she was, she realised that the urge to kiss him, to taste him was right there. Like lifting a teacloth cover off a poorly concealed cake she'd been hankering over for too long.

And then she dropped her gaze again. Down the front of his jacket, which did little to disguise the well-built chest beneath, and the lower abs that she'd traced with her fingers, and then her tongue, that night back in the hotel.

And suddenly she was staring straight at the part of him that she should be looking at the least. The part that got her the hottest.

The vehicle lurched without warning, and Mattie shot her hand up to brace herself on the inside of the roof as they bounced along, helpless to stop her legs from banging against Kane's.

He lowered his hand, out of sight, to rest it on her thigh, steadying her. But the contact was scorching, branding her from the inside out. It was insane how badly she wanted to slide down her seat and make Kane's hand move higher. More centrally.

She wouldn't. Of course she wouldn't. But the need that pounded through her was incredible. Almost overwhelming.

'Sorry, ma'am…sir,' the young corporal designated as their driver apologised for the third time. 'The ground is a lot boggier than we thought.'

'Yeah, the map will show a lot of things, but it won't pick up weather-affected terrain,' Kane muttered as Mattie was flung towards him again. 'The place was probably bone dry a month ago.'

She braced her hand tighter against the roof, trying to give herself support. If she got thrown around any more, she was in danger of landing face first in Kane's lap, which was hardly going to help their efforts to ignore whatever this *thing* was between them. And they'd been doing so well over the past couple of days.

Yeah, keep lying to yourself if it makes you feel better, needled a wry voice inside her head.

Because, for her, every touch was reigniting the sparks she'd told herself she'd snuffed out.

Suddenly the vehicle wallowed heavily, and despite her best efforts Mattie pitched forward, slamming into the solid wall that was Kane's chest. Only his hands reaching out to grab her and steady her against him stopped her from sliding painfully to the floor.

'Thanks,' she muttered, wanting to move but unable to.

It was too intoxicating to stay here, pressed against him. She could feel his heart beating, strong and slightly too fast, echoing the pulse that drummed at her neck. Making her wonder if he could feel everything that she felt.

If he was as close to the edge as she was, so that a moment like this could undo all the good work they'd managed by avoiding each other the past couple of days.

'You okay, ma'am?'

The corporal's voice sliced through Mattie's thoughts, jolting her back into action. Hastily, she reached out and tried to lever herself up.

Only when she braced her hand this time, it was against a hard, muscled thigh—something decidedly *Kane*-like.

Shocked, she snatched her hand back as though burned, fire racing to her cheeks. It was one thing knowing he was as affected as she was, but it was something else feeling the indisputable proof of it so hot, and full of promise, against the palm of her hand.

Knowing she couldn't do a single thing about it.

'I'm sorry... I...'

'It's fine,' he cut her off tersely, jerking his head towards their driver in silent caution, but it was the look of intensity in his expression that reached into her chest and tugged. 'I suggest we stop and get out. Maybe have a look for ourselves rather than suffering this.'

Mattie fought to wrest her tongue from the roof of her parched mouth.

'I agree. At least it will afford us an opportunity to look for higher ground. It wouldn't take more than a few inches to get us out of this marsh.'

And give Kane and her a chance to get out of earshot of the young corporal, who would have to stay with the vehicle. Although what she was supposed to say after... *that* was unclear.

'Shall I stop, ma'am?'

'Yes, Corporal. Stop here.'

He obeyed, apparently only too eager to end the torture for himself, and Mattie took the chance to jump down from the back, giving Kane a moment longer to sort himself out.

Grabbing a day sack, she started to head off across the ground, knowing he would catch up with her when he was ready.

'The buildings should be over there…' She indicated a few moments later as he stepped alongside her. 'Just over that small rise.'

Her cheeks still felt like they were on fire, but there was no need to prolong the moment. In truth, the best thing they could do would be to get this mission done and over with. It was increasingly clear to her that the longer she and Kane spent together, the stronger their attraction was growing.

And the more she didn't want it to stop.

Forcing herself back into the moment, she turned to speak to Kane just as he was peering into the distance.

'It doesn't look promising.'

'Ground conditions are less than ideal,' she noted.

'For you medics perhaps,' he noted evenly. 'This is why the infantry come to places like this. To train over all kinds of terrain.'

'Yeah, yeah, you're all as hard as nails, I know.' And before she could stop herself, she was teasing him again.

Crossing that line. Again.

Biting her tongue, she concentrated on walking over the uneven terrain, reaching the top of the rise. Another step and she'd see over the low brow.

'Oh.'

Damn.

'That's disappointing.' Kane blew out heavily as they both stopped. 'You could lose whole tanks in those depressions. The helicopters will never be able to land.'

He was right. The ground had folds in it that would

never have been picked up on the map. Worse than that, though, was the fact that piles of stones lay where the collection of buildings was supposed to have been.

'They're more than just ruins.' Mattie exhaled. 'They've practically crumbled to the ground. There's no shelter there for any medical triage area. I don't mind rewriting scenarios on the fly, but there really ought to be something they can use as makeshift shelter.'

'Yeah, this location is a dud. Shall we try the next? The next one we identified is only a couple of clicks that way on the other side of that wood.' He gestured to a treeline further into the distance. 'We could walk it, or get back to the main track and see how far it takes us around by vehicle.'

There looked to be a path leading into the wood, or they could skirt around it as it wasn't too extensive. But time was running out and the vehicle was probably the best option.

Mattie worried at her lips with her teeth. She wanted to take a moment. It was just a bit too intense in that four-by-four right now, with Kane too damn close for comfort and the corporal seeing her every blush and flush, like there was something going on.

Especially when she and Kane had been doing so well at ensuring there was absolutely *nothing* going on at all.

'You want to just walk on a bit further?' he asked quietly.

She nodded, grateful that she didn't have to say anything for him to understand. They walked in silence to the ruins, and he stopped on a rock whilst she pretended to take a tour around them. Catching her breath.

'We'll find thd next location and confirm it as the new scenario site, then we'll be back at camp by nightfall,' Kane assured her as they finally headed back to the four-by-four.

'Right,' she agreed.

She hoped so. They'd packed for staying out for the

night, and normally she would have looked forward to the opportunity to be away from everything—even her beloved hospital—for a night.

But sleeping so close to Kane, with some random corporal acting like some kind of eighteenth-century chaperone—not that the poor kid knew it—wasn't going to be something she relished.

Climbing back into the rear of the vehicle, she shoved one of the bergens to one side and rammed her legs into the space, telling herself that it was for the best. At least this way no contact with Kane would mean no temptation. And that could only be a good thing.

The vehicle rumbled off, their young driver briefed on the new co-ordinates, but they hadn't been going for more than ten minutes when Mattie felt the vehicle pull to a halt. Carefully she leaned over the back of the seat.

'Everything all right, Corporal?'

'There are two tracks on the ground, ma'am, but only one on the map.'

Kane was out and taking a look before she could respond.

'My instinct would be to take the higher one.' He shrugged as he returned. 'But there's no clear indication which is best.'

Given the boggy nature of the ground, that would have been her instinct, too.

'Agreed.' She nodded. 'But if we need to get out and continue on foot, I have no issues with that.'

'Understood,' Kane confirmed, hauling himself into the front seat this time, and taking the lead as any other WO2 might have done.

Sometimes, Mattie decided, there were definite disadvantages to being the CO. Not least the fact that it wasn't always easy to just get in there and get your hands dirty.

And then, without warning, the four-by-four lurched

sickeningly, throwing Mattie from her seat and almost slamming her head against the metal frames on the side of the vehicle. When they jerked to a halt, the off roader was at a worrying angle.

'Are you all right, ma'am?' The corporal's agitated voice finally broke into the silence. 'Sir?'

Mattie had no idea how she forced her protesting muscles back into action and push herself back up and onto her own seat. It didn't mean she could talk, though.

'Fine,' Kane confirmed after half a beat. 'What about you?'

'Um…yeah…' the young lad began before catching himself. 'Yes, I think so, sir.'

Kane reached for the back door, swinging it open.

'Okay, let's assess the damage, shall we?'

Gathering herself together, Mattie followed him, leaping down on legs that she told herself weren't shaking—and if they were, it was only because of the violence of the accident and nothing whatsoever to do with Kane.

And when she turned back to look, she almost convinced herself that it was true. A rear wheel of the four-by-four had apparently opened up a narrow fissure, not even deep enough for a person to fall into but certainly deep enough to trap a wheel. So whilst there was no imminent danger of it opening up and pulling the vehicle in, there was clearly no way they were going to be able to drive out of the situation.

'It wasn't on the map, either ma'am,' the corporal told her anxiously.

'No, I imagine not. These prairies are extensive and not every square inch of it will have been mapped. We'll get to safety and call it in.'

'I suggest we try and push it out, ma'am,' Kane concluded after an initial assessment, before locking his gaze with hers. 'If that doesn't work, we can radio for backup.'

With anyone else she probably would have doubted their ability to succeed but, then, anyone else wasn't Kane. Brown eyes held hers as something lurched in Mattie's chest. She ruthlessly quashed it.

'You look the strongest, Mr Wheeler, perhaps you should take the rear.' Her voice was miraculously even and controlled. She'd never been more grateful for all her years of training. 'Corporal, you open the driver door and take that side, and I'll take this side.'

'Yes, ma'am.' The corporal scurried back around to the driver's door, opening it wide and holding the main body of the vehicle across from Mattie, as she did the same.

'Mr Wheeler, if you'd like to count us in when you're ready.'

'All right. One, two, three...'

The three of them pushed. The four-by-four rocked promisingly but didn't move.

'Perhaps you'd like to release the handbrake, Corporal,' Kane remarked dryly.

'Yes, sir. Sorry, sir.' The young lad went a fiery red and leaned into the cab. 'All done, sir.'

'Again, on three,' Kane said.

On his count, Mattie threw her full force into pushing the heavy vehicle but there was no doubt in her mind that it was Kane's input that ultimately, miraculously had the four-by-four moving. Not far, but enough to get the fourth wheel onto solid ground, although Mattie couldn't imagine them being able to push it much further given the rough terrain.

'Corporal, do you want to jump in and start the engine.' It was less of a request from Kane and more of a command. 'Move to the outbuilding over there, as we know that's safe ground. I suggest we follow on foot, Major.'

'I concur.' Mattie dipped her head, wishing she didn't

feel such a thrill at the idea of even a few moments alone with Kane.

Especially after that...*moment* when she'd been flung into his arms.

The young lad obeyed and within moments he was driving the four-by-four carefully over the terrain, leaving Mattie and Kane to follow on foot.

'You can call it in from the shelter,' she muttered quietly, in some kind of half-hearted attempt to keep things professional.

As though it could keep her head in the right place. Kane didn't seem to have read the unspoken memo.

'You okay, Mattie?'

'Fine,' she replied quickly. Too quickly. Too tightly.

'You got thrown around quite badly back there.'

'I said I'm fine.' She could see his head swivel towards her in her peripheral vision, but she ignored it.

She *was* fine...if she didn't count the way Kane seemed to constantly get under her skin.

'Have it your own way.' He sounded more amused than irritated.

'There's a bit of a grinding noise, ma'am,' the corporal suddenly called, as he stopped the vehicle. 'I just want to have a check.'

And then things happened so fast that Mattie barely had time to notice.

The lad jumped out of the four-by-four, slipping slightly as he landed. Spinning his body around, he reached out to grab the bonnet and the vehicle—its handbrake evidently not having been applied—began to roll back slightly.

As the corporal struggled to get traction on the wet grass and pull himself out of the way of the wheel, he twisted again, this time awkwardly, and then there was a loud cracking sound and a scream.

'He's broken his leg,' Mattie ground out, straightening up and beginning to run down the hill, Kane's boots pounding the ground next to her.

'Don't go in there until I've secured the vehicle,' he commanded.

As Mattie headed for the casualty, Kane yanked open the vehicle door and snatched on the handbrake. The bone sticking through the lad's leg and trousers were obvious the moment she arrived.

'Bring my medical grab bag,' she ordered, barely glancing up at Kane as she concentrated on the corporal. 'Okay, Daryl, isn't it?'

The lad made what sounded like a confirmation, though it wasn't clear over his cries of pain.

'Okay, Daryl, you have a compound fracture so what I'm going to do is stem the bleeding, immobilise the area, and see if we can't reduce your pain. But first I just want to check you for any other injuries. Does it hurt anywhere else?'

Quickly she began to check over his body. She suspected it was just the fracture of the lower leg, but she didn't want to miss any internal bleeding caused by some impact she hadn't quite seen.

'All right, Daryl, mate, it's going to be okay, Doc's treating you now.' Kane returned with her bag then knelt next to the corporal, taking his hand and beginning to talk, his low voice calm and soothing. Then he turned to her. 'What do you want me to do?'

'Can you get some scissors and cut his trousers? I want to pack this field dressing around the bone to staunch the bleeding and protect the injury, then elevate the limb.'

Dutifully Kane searched through her bag, quickly producing a pair of scissors and some field dressing kits. As he cut the trousers, she pulled off the soldier's boot and sock and checked for a pulse in the foot, relieved when she found it. At least the neurovascular state of his leg was good. She had known some soldiers who had ended up needing the foot amputated because a leg fracture had resulted in circulatory deterioration.

Pulling the field dressing apart, she lowered it around the protruding bone, working quickly and efficiently as she pressed it to the wound to staunch the bleeding.

'Right, apply pressure here,' she told him. 'Then I can pack the wound.'

'His breathing is becoming rapid,' Kane noted quietly, so that the young lad couldn't hear, and Mattie nodded grimly.

'His colour and temperature aren't looking too good either. I'm concerned about hypovolaemia.'

Ideally, she would give the lad oxygen, but she didn't have any with her. But she could give an intravenous saline solution to replenish his fluids, and she still needed to splint the leg.

'There's a box splint in the cab,' she told Kane. 'But I'd prefer to put his leg into traction. Can you see if there are any long sticks or branches by those trees? I need one longer than the other, one to run on the outside from the chest down to the ankle, and the other to run on the inside from the groin.'

'Diameter?'

'Enough to take some strain, maybe around five centimetres or so?'

'On it,' Kane confirmed, heading quickly towards the trees.

She plunged back into her med pack, talking to Daryl all the while. If she wanted to manipulate the corporal's leg she was going to need to administer some pain relief, and there was a morphine injector in her kit. And prepping a few bandages to use as ties would save time.

Kane was back quicker than she had hoped, bringing with him a decent selection of thick sticks.

'Great,' she approved, selecting the best, straightest two. 'Now, I'm going to need you to grab his ankle and pull the leg down.'

As Kane obliged, Mattie quickly set up the traction, constantly checking for signs of neurovascular compromise each time she made an adjustment. And then they were done, and whilst Kane called it in, she focused on keeping the injured man warm, and talking, reassuring him all the while.

'Okay, the heli-med will be here in ten. But we're going to need to get him off this patch of ground. They won't be able to land here.'

Mattie glanced around quickly.

'I don't want to put him in that vehicle, not the way it will toss him around. We're going to have to tab him out.'

'Understood,' Kane confirmed. 'I'll get the stretcher from the cab.'

By the time they'd loaded the corporal on the stretcher and carried him out of the dip to more level ground, she could already hear the helicopter in the distance.

Instinctively, Mattie stood over her patient, protecting him as best she could from the downdraught of the rotors, waiting as her guys jumped off the back and hurried over to carry out her handover with a few additional instructions besides. Before long, they were loading the corporal into the heli.

'Will you be returning with us, ma'am?'

She could feel Kane's eyes on her. Boring into her back. She didn't dare turn. Still, as she shook her head, she was grateful for the ability to keep her tone light yet professional.

'No,' she confirmed. 'We still need to determine the location for the new medical phase of the exercise. The first two locations didn't turn out to be appropriate.'

'Should we send out another driver?'

Mattie forced a bright smile.

'No, I'm sure Mr Wheeler can drive us.'

'Of course, ma'am.' His voice rumbled through her as potent as ever, but she made herself ignore it.

She ignored the niggling voice asking whether there wasn't a tiny part of her that was welcoming this opportunity to be alone with Kane again. Even though the rational part of her brain just said that she was courting disaster.

'Jolly good.' She offered a firm nod. 'Then I anticipate returning to the hospital tomorrow.'

'Jolly good?' Kane rumbled as the team jumped back onto the heli and it started to take off. 'I don't think I've ever heard you use those words before.'

'Leave it alone, Kane.'

'Jolly good,' he continued, without a hint of contrition.

She wanted to chastise him, but Mattie found she couldn't. She felt light suddenly. Free. The young corporal had been a decent lad, but it had been such a confining situation with Kane that she'd felt under scrutiny the whole time.

Maybe now she didn't feel her every word could be analysed she wouldn't feel so edgy.

Yeah. Right.

'Listen, the accident, not that it was anyone's fault,' she added hastily, 'has put us a couple of hours behind. The sooner we find and reach this third location and assess it, the sooner we can get back to the hospital.'

'You and I both know that isn't happening tonight,' Kane replied in a low voice.

And there was no reason for that to send such a thrill rippling through her.

No reason at all.

Mattie watched wordlessly as the chopper disappeared towards the horizon, more to rein in her racing heartbeat than anything else. Finally, she turned back.

They were alone. Just the two of them.

There was no one else around for miles and miles. The ultimate test of their resolve to concentrate on their jobs and resist each other.

'Well, *Mr Wheeler*,' she said pointedly, since there was no logical reason for them not to resort to first names as the corporal was no longer with them. Still, she softened her words with a smile. 'Perhaps you're right, but shall we continue? I'd rather not stay out here in the middle of... *nothing* all night.'

'We shall, *ma'am*.' He dipped his head as he swung up into the driver's seat, acknowledging the point she was indirectly making.

She climbed up into the passenger seat and turned to look at him, only for him to grin. That familiar, wolfish smile which made her imagine those straight, white teeth against her bare skin.

Doing things to her.

'Kane...'

'Actually, *ma'am*...' his grin pulled wider, teasing her '...I rather thought you might walk ahead of the vehicle back to the track.'

'You want me to walk us out of here?'

'Just to check the ground is solid enough for a heavy four-by-four,' he confirmed.

Mattie narrowed her eyes at him. It was a sound point but she just couldn't help thinking he was relishing the moment.

'Unless you want to drive, of course.'

They both knew, as CO, she couldn't do that. It was an odd quirk of the British army that a commissioned officer wasn't permitted to drive themselves around in military vehicles.

Any accident—even the one they'd just had involving the young corporal—would result in being called in front of the driver's commanding officer for an investigation pending disciplinary action. For the corporal, the CO would be his own officer-in-command, a major. For an NCO as senior as Kane, his CO would be a lieutenant-colonel.

But she, as a commissioned officer, would be called in front of the brigade commander—a general—and that could be the difference between her getting a promotion or not.

If she'd no driver and no choice, that would be different, especially in an exercise area. But when she was standing right in front of an NCO...well, it was pointless to risk her career just to prove a point to Kane Wheeler.

Glowering at him, because he was enjoying himself rather too much, Mattie swung back down and made a point of shutting the vehicle door as she turned her back. Not a slam, but loud enough to rock the four-by-four. She could hear Kane's deep, rich laugh as she stomped across the uneven terrain and stepped out in front of the four-by-four. Then, watching each step but more conscious of his eyes on her backside, she began to walk back to the track, making sure the ground was firm enough to take the weight of the vehicle as she went.

And if she put a little extra pizzaz into the swing of her hips, thrusting her hands into her pockets to hug the otherwise unflattering material tighter to her backside, *so what?*

Besides, Kane probably hadn't even noticed. He'd barely looked at her twice in the past couple of days and she hated to admit that it was galling to realise that he'd been finding it so easy to ignore the attraction that still burned low in her, whether he was around or not.

So, really, why not sashay a little? After all, what was the worst that could happen?

CHAPTER TEN

CONCENTRATE ON THE **damned ground**.

Gripping the wheel tighter, Kane fought to drag his gaze from that peachy derrière and back to the task in hand. The last thing he wanted to do was repeat the mistake the corporal had made, but Mattie was hardly making it easy for him to stay focused. Especially because the fading light had caused him to have to turn the lights on, illuminating her—and her delectable rear—like a Christmas tree.

Worse, he didn't *want* to stay focused. He just wanted Mattie. And the more time they spent together, the stronger that emotion was becoming. It had been like a slow burn from the moment they'd agreed to keep things *strictly professional*. In some ways, he'd welcomed the challenge—being this close to her but controlling the tumbling desires. Proving to himself that he could. Like some exquisite torture.

But now it was just plain torture and there was nothing *exquisite* about it. Being cooped up with her in the back of the four-by-four for the past day, her leg or hand brushing him every time that corporal had driven over a bump—and there were plenty of them out here, in this rough terrain—had been enough to kill him. He'd spent most of the day uncomfortably hard.

And now she was swinging that backside from side to

side, practically driving him insane. He couldn't get them back to the main track quickly enough.

'Get in,' he growled to her, leaning out of the driver's window as soon as the vehicle jerked from the rough off-road terrain to the slightly less rough track.

'Problem?' She turned slowly, sweetly, before saunter-ing around to the passenger door and pulling herself up gracefully.

He wasn't fooled. So she *had* known what she was doing. Was it wrong that it gave him a kick, low in his gut, to know that she'd done it deliberately? That she'd *wanted* to turn him on? The corners of his mouth tugged upwards.

'No problem for me. You?'

She'd been doing such a good job of acting profession-ally over the last couple of days that he'd really started to believe she wasn't finding it anywhere near as difficult to resist temptation as he was.

Her gaze caught his. Sparkling. Fun. The Mattie he'd never been able to refuse. Never *wanted* to.

'None at all.' She grinned, and a lick of heat swept over him.

He could just stop the vehicle right here. No one was around. The temptation was almost overwhelming. Kane scrabbled to keep a grip on reality.

'That said, I want to check the underside of this vehi-cle to make sure no real damage was done in the accident, but the light is already fading. And out here it fades fast.'

'Oh, do you think there was damage?' she asked seri-ously, the sexual tension between them mercifully, regret-tably broken.

'I don't know.' He navigated the uneven ground around the hill. 'But it wouldn't hurt to check. Preferably on flat-ter ground and whilst we still have some light.'

Mattie peered through the windscreen, the land begin-ning to flatten and fall away as they crested the hill.

'Wait, what's that?'

He stopped the vehicle and followed the direction of her gaze, squinting to see better.

'Looks like a collection of old farm buildings,' he hazarded, turning as Mattie looked up from consulting the map.

'There looks to be something of a track although it isn't marked on the map. But this place is so vast not everything can be. Want to check it out? It's a damn sight closer than the area we were originally heading for.'

He revved the engine gently and guided the vehicle until they were on the new track. If nothing else, it certainly looked like a better place to spend the night than out in the open. Not that his mind really wanted to go there at this moment. Anyway, he'd been getting concerned that they wouldn't make it there before sunset, which made this a potentially better stop-over.

In silence they made their way to the cluster of buildings, somewhat reassured by the directness of the only slightly overgrown track. Pulling up outside it and climbing out, they made their way around the outhouses, which were in varying states of ruin.

'You know, this might actually make a good location for the new pre-phase,' Mattie said consideringly after several minutes. 'One of the buildings around that side still has its roof pretty much intact so it would an ideal spot to set up the triage and stabilisation section.'

'It isn't in a bad position for defending against tactical fire,' agreed Kane, circling back around the buildings as he headed back to the vehicle. 'And we already know there's an ideal landing zone back down the hill, where they can tab their casualties out.'

'It isn't too far off the designated route for the infantry?' she checked.

Kane slid the map out of his pocket, laying it on the bonnet to check.

'Less than a klick, so it's no big deal to bring them over this way slightly. See?'

She jogged across the path and peered over his shoulder, so close that he could feel her breast against his arm. The hear seared his skin even through the jacket and he heard her catch her breath. Then his brain cracked and went blank.

'Yes,' she managed thickly, refusing to meet his eyes. 'I see.'

'I'd like to drive it to be certain, but not at this hour.'

'So we're out here for the night,' she remarked, and he found himself listening for any indication of whether she was happy about that or concerned.

But her tone was frustratingly even, giving nothing away, so instead he tried to gather the map up without snatching, only to end up making a meal of folding it back up.

He cleared his throat.

'If we get the four-by-four into that first ruin, the ground's flat enough for me to check underneath.'

'Fine. I'll grab a bergen from the back and start setting up camp.'

Peeling off his jacket and hooking it over the wing mirror, Kane began working on the vehicle. Slowly, methodically giving himself a chance to get his head back in focus as much as anything else. He could hear the bustling sounds as Mattie set things up on the other side of the crumbling wall and it was almost…homely. Was that good thing or a bad one? He worked steadily, his head torch allowing him to finally complete the task. And there was nothing left but to rejoin her.

His heart kicked stubbornly.

'Good timing.' She glanced up as he walked through the half-doorway.

She'd laid out her bedroll and sleeping bag and had lit a fire for warmth. A small pile of logs sat next to it so they could keep feeding it through the night, which he had to admit wasn't a bad idea as the temperatures could drop considerably out here at night.

She even had a couple of rat packs by a gas burner, and he heard himself teasing her before he could stop.

'Cooking me dinner? From the kid who needed me to teach her to boil water?'

'Don't get used to it,' she quipped. 'I've left you to sort out your own bedroll and sleeping bag.'

Stepping forward, he dropped his rucksack and jacket on the other side of the fire from hers.

'Fair enough.'

'You know you have oil on your T-shirt?'

'I didn't know that, no.' He glanced down before peeling it up and over his head.

At least he had a spare in his bag. But when he retrieved it, standing up tall to pull it on, he became aware of Mattie staring intently at him.

Checking him out.

The air around them became heavy. Charged. And Kane couldn't help it, he slowed his movements, taking his time, loving the way her eyes darkened and her nostrils flared slightly as she drank in the sight of him. Like he was as pool of fresh, clear water in the middle of a desert.

The blood rushed through him. No one had ever had him as on edge as this one woman.

'Matz.'

She snapped her head up, her cheeks reddening slightly, which only fired him up all the more. Did that stain creep below her shirt? Over her perfect breasts? If he walked over there and hauled her into his arms, how long would it be before he could find out?

Because he wanted to. He wanted his hands all over her, closely followed by his mouth. From the elegant curve of her neck to the creamy swell of her breasts. And from the smooth expanse of her abdomen to the honeyed sweetness between her legs.

Lord, how he wanted to taste her again.

Realisation punched him in the gut—and lower—and he swung sharply away before his traitorous body betrayed him.

Being here alone with Mattie and in the middle of nowhere was a bad idea. Because out here there was no one to keep them in check. It felt like the brakes were off and he was already slipping down the hill. Slowly at first, but it wouldn't be long until he was careening out of control.

The last time he'd allowed himself to be out of control had been around twenty years ago, when he'd been stupid enough to let his brothers use him. When he'd been stupid enough to cover for them after he'd realised what they had done.

When he'd joined the army—when it had been that or face some kind of prosecution—he'd grabbed the opportunity to reinvent himself, to build a new life for himself with both hands. He'd sworn there and then that he would never do anything to jeopardise that, and he never had. Not in fourteen years.

But every time he was with Mathilda Brigham, all that went out the window whilst his common sense convoy became a runaway train.

And a crash was inevitable.

Mattie glowered into the fire and felt edgy. Restless. Unruly. No one had ever made her feel as wanton as Kane did. As he always had done.

She'd been fighting this pull ever since he'd walked into her field hospital, but she knew she'd been gradually losing the battle. And now they were here, alone, in the middle of nowhere, with no one around. It wasn't as though anyone was going to sneak up on them in a tank or a chopper.

It was just Kane and her.

And the darkness that had settled over them like a blanket, an inky blue, snuggly fleece, flecked with stars that shimmered and winked in the unending sky, seemed to add to the sense of intimacy. Out here there was no pollution. No light. No noise. Only the moonlight, slicing through the broken tiles in the roof above them and bathing the room in an almost romantic light.

Almost magic. Just as the air around them was thick with everything they weren't saying. Everything they weren't doing. And even though Mattie knew that they shouldn't, she couldn't seem to bring herself to stop.

Or, worse, to care about stopping.

Her pulse beat, wild and fast, at her throat. His eyes flickered to it, clearly able to see how he affected her as he swallowed. It appeared that her body wasn't alone in fighting a thousand desires that tumbled through her.

She *had* to resist him. She was an acting *colonel*, for pity's sake.

'I can't believe we've both been in for over a decade,' Mattie muttered. 'We must have been in the same theatres of war, surely? Yet we've never run into each other before.'

'Why would we? Infantry are front line, medical aren't.' He lifted his shoulders. 'And I've been in camps with ten, twenty, thirty thousand soldiers. Would it really be that surprising? Besides, what if we *had* crossed paths? What would that change?'

She tipped her head to one side thoughtfully as there was something in his tone she couldn't quite pinpoint.

'Perhaps not. But surely we would have at least *heard* the other's name mentioned. Realised.'

'I already knew you were in,' he pointed out. 'That was never an unknown for me. You, Hayd and your father.'

She paused sadly for a moment.

'Not my father. Not recently, anyway.'

'His Alzheimer's is really that bad?'

She could feel the hot prickling behind her eyes. Hating herself for the weakness, but it had come out of nowhere, almost blindsiding her. A rational corner of her brain was trying to say something, possibly that it was the tension of the last few days of suppressing this insane chemistry between herself and Kane that had really got to her.

Warning her that engaging in personal conversation with him was the last thing she should be doing if she wanted to avoid crossing the line with him again, the way they had back in her office that first day.

But she wasn't listening. Whether because she couldn't, or more because she didn't *want* to, Mattie couldn't be sure.

'I hadn't seen him as often as I might have liked. I'd always been too busy, but I guess that's a poor excuse.' She waited for Kane to answer, but he didn't. 'Maybe a perverse part of me felt as though I was being like him by saying the same.'

'Does it help?'

'The opposite.' She pursed her lips in an effort to control the welling sadness, 'I feel like I've let him down. Been selfish.'

The prickling was getting painful now and she dropped her eyes to stare into the fire, as though the dancing flames could somehow dry all the tears before they fell.

She heard a shuffle, and felt Kane moving beside her, his strong arms wrapping around her and pulling her into the safety of his chest. And, for a moment, she felt safe, and seventeen, all over again.

She had no idea how long they stayed there, she warm in his arms.

'So where have you been? I mean, which tours?'

He named a few places. Something in his tone told her that they were operational tours that he was happy to forget but which, sometimes in the dead of the night, his brain remembered in all too startling clarity, and he would wake up in a cold sweat.

A sensation she knew well enough.

And then he mentioned another tour, the worst tour she'd ever known, and she froze in his arms.

'I was there, too. What year?'

For a moment, Kane hesitated, then he told her. It was as though an icy cold hand was creeping down her spine, spreading chill everywhere it touched.

'That was hell on earth,' she muttered thickly. 'There was an ambush in an abandoned village. Our guys went in to get the women and children but...'

She couldn't go on. Kane merely grunted but didn't speak. She realised he couldn't. His heart was pounding in his chest, thundering under her ear.

She lifted her head and stared into the flames and, for a moment, all she could hear was the crackling of the fire and a ragged voice. It took her a few moments to realise it was her own.

'I saw some of the guys in there. I didn't even think you'd make it out at one point.'

The air was thick with tension. A thousand memories, many of them bleak.

'We nearly didn't. We were pretty much pinned down, taking heavy fire with some really serious casualties. No one could get in to us, and we couldn't get out. And then, suddenly, this sandstorm came in and we decided it was all or nothing. We managed to get past the enemy, even got some distance away, though not far enough for any ambulance to risk getting into us. But then some crazy pilot flew in a chopper with a MERT team, led by the biggest badass army trauma doctor I've ever seen, to recover our two wounded.'

She blinked at him slowly, could feel the shock beginning to cloud her face.

He couldn't be talking about her...could he?

'The med team had barely got our buddies on board when the enemy tracked us, but the doc wouldn't get on until the rest of her team were safely on board. We held them off long enough for the chopper to get off the ground, but I saw the doctor get clipped by a round in the back of her leg just as she leapt on board.'

'Is that so?' Mattie asked faintly, her gaze caught with his. She wasn't sure if either of them were even daring to breathe, but she couldn't stop her hand sliding down to her calf to the scar from that bullet wound. The scar he'd felt that first night together back in the hotel.

Did he know that he was talking about her? Did he realise?

And if so, had he recognised her back in that hellhole? Because she'd had absolutely no idea that, crouched down by her heli—trying to give enough covering fire so that she and her team could get the injured soldiers out—one of the other men still fighting had been Kane.

Her Kane.

Leaving those guys on the ground had been the worst feeling she'd ever had to deal with—knowing she was leaving them to their inevitable deaths. There was no way they were going to make it out alive, but the chopper had been tiny. Too small for anyone but her team and the two casualties.

Few things haunted her—one couldn't afford to let them in this job—but that day did. Even now, she could remember that sensation as the adrenalin had kicked in and she—

her whole team—had been determined to save the lives of those two injured soldiers. To make sure their buddies hadn't died for nothing.

She'd had no choice—not that the knowledge helped. Nausea swelled within her.

'Like I said, a hell of a leader,' he said quietly. 'Risking their lives to save our buddies. It gave us the morale boost we needed. We just threw ourselves into that firefight knowing that even if we went down, at least two of us had made it out.'

'I heard the firefight went on for eleven hours,' she told him softly.

'Yeah, about that. But because of you we were determined not to give up. And then suddenly it was all over and we'd won.'

'I know. We couldn't believe it.'

'Neither could we.' He grinned, a bitter-sweet twist of his mouth. 'But want to know what the cherry on the icing on that admittedly bloodied cake was?'

'Tell me.'

'Both our buddies made it. Thanks to you.'

'Thanks to *you*.' She shook her head. 'We weren't the guys who tabbed out of an ambush, in the middle of a sandstorm, with two stretchers.'

'And what difference would it have made if you and the pilot hadn't brought the chopper through with the MERT team?' he countered. 'No one else was coming. We knew that. As far as the guys and I were concerned, that godforsaken, abandoned village in the middle of nowhere was going to be our final resting place.'

'We kept up with your team.' Mattie nodded. 'We couldn't believe you'd got out.'

She could remember the shock as her team had heard the news back in the field hospital—such as it had been on that tour. An initial numbness. And then a feeling of absolute euphoria. It had been like their own personal miracle and they'd ridden that high for the rest of the tour.

'But we did.'

'Yes, you did,' she agreed fiercely, pulling out of his arms until she was sitting back on her heels, facing him.

She wasn't sure whose gaze was trapped in whose. Frankly, she didn't much care.

'Life is so precious, Kane,' she whispered. 'I know it, and yet I forget it. But every now and then something rams it home to me and I realise that we have to make the most out of this short time we have.'

'And everything we said back in your office?' he bit out, his hoarse voice scratching over her.

Inside her.

She swallowed, her head dipping closer to his. Inviting him without a word.

'Mattie.' He breathed her name and it sent charges of electricity through her. 'I need you to be sure about this. I want to hear it.'

'You don't need to hear anything, Kane.' She barely recognised her own voice. 'Don't they say that actions speaker louder than words?'

CHAPTER ELEVEN

THE SLOW BURN that had smouldered in him ever since he'd walked into her office in her field hospital had turned into a full inferno, ripping through him as though nothing could ever douse it.

As though he never *wanted* anything to douse it.

He was dimly aware of a muffled voice, deep inside his brain, warning him that if they did this, there could be no going back. That they could no longer pretend they were beating this…*thing* that arced between them. They could no longer profess that their army careers were the most important thing that mattered to them.

Everything would change. It would have to.

If he were a stronger man, a better man, he surely would have resisted. For both of them. Got them through this weak moment now that they'd found themselves alone in the middle of the deserted prairies where there was no chance of anyone intruding on them.

But he wasn't a *better* man. He never had been. It had been his distinct lack of respect for the law that had brought him to the army in the first instance—even if he hadn't knowingly committed the crime, a good man would have gone straight to the police when he'd realised what his brothers were doing. It was probably why a part of him had always felt like an imposter all these years, even when his career had started to soar.

Especially when his career had started to soar.

So now, as the moonlight sliced through the broken roof of the old building lending the space an ethereal glow, bathing Mattie in a romantic light, he felt a fervour pouring through his whole body. Dark and powerful. Filling him up and making him ache.

Making him yearn when he'd never *yearned* in his life.

Except for Mattie.

Kane stopped thinking, he didn't allow himself another moment to second-guess, he simply reached out and traced that exquisitely perfect jawline the way he'd been aching to do for days. For all his life.

And he revelled in the feel of her skin, so smooth and soft, beneath the rough pad of his thumb. He wanted her. He couldn't keep away from her. Even when he knew that they were bad for each other. Even though he understood that there could never be a future.

Because neither of them would be prepared to walk away from the only careers they had ever known. Not even for each other.

But right here, right now, he was staring into those mesmerising blue eyes of hers, which were darker than usual, and glittering at him. And even though logic told him that it was a bad idea, and that nothing had changed since the last time they'd been alone, he didn't care. It was nonsensical, and reckless, but he felt as though everything was going to be all right as long as the two of them were together.

Because, really, when it came down to it, being apart hadn't allowed either of them to move on emotionally, had it?

Sliding his hand to cradle the back of her head, he hauled Mattie towards him, revelling in the way that she moved so willingly, pressing her body against his so that heat seared through the layers of clothing that separated them.

A part of him ached to tear them off, but Kane refused to rush. He indulged himself as she tilted her head back for him, allowing him to angle her head just right. He indulged himself as his tongue scraped hers, another shot of desire racing between them. And he indulged himself when she made those soft yet greedy noises in the back of her throat.

He had never been able to get enough of those sounds. He wasn't sure he ever would.

With his free hand he traced the line of her elegant neck, over her shoulders and down her arm, and it didn't matter that she was clad in the heavy material of her uniform, he could still remember how soft her skin felt.

Kane took his time kissing her. Tasting her. Teasing her. He was a man trained in any number of weapons, but right now those weapons were his mouth, his tongue, his teeth, and he intended to lay waste to Mattie with every one of them.

But it was harder to keep his control than he liked when she began winding her arms around his neck and moving to straddle his lap, making his body tighten. Ache.

'Did you think you were going to get it all your own way, Kane?' she growled huskily, hardly helping matters. 'Perhaps you're forgetting who is in control here.'

'You might be in control of this little recce party, *ma'am*,' he teased, dragged her lower lip between his teeth. 'But I'm going to be the one running tonight's entertainment.'

And then, before she could answer, he dropped his head to nuzzle at her neck. Kissing her, teasing her with his teeth, loving it when she dropped her head back, one of her hands laced through his hair, the other gripping his shoulder.

She tasted so damned good. So damned right. And the moonlight streamed in through the old ruin as if it, too, agreed.

And then he was moving his lips over skin, grazing her neck a little with his teeth as he made his slow, meandering way down to that sensitive hollow by her collarbone. He fought to keep control, to take his time. As if those little needy sounds she was making weren't driving him insanely wild with need. As if he didn't actually *hurt* with the urge to simply slide straight inside her. But not yet.

Not yet.

Slowly, deliberately, as though he was unwrapping a precious gift, Kane reached for the zip of her jacket and slowly began to lower it. The sound was especially loud, and loaded, in the silent night air, and somehow that only seemed to make the air pull tighter with delicious expectation.

Then, finally, he shucked the jacket off Mattie's shoulders, easing it down her arms and perhaps indulging a little too much in the way it made her straighten up and push her breasts harder against his chest. His mouth teased at her neck as he felt for the hem of her T-shirt and lifted that too, unhurriedly, up and over her head as she lifted her arms in unspoken compliance. And then there was only her pretty, lacy bra, doing little to cover the acres of lush, smooth skin that had haunted his nights for…*ever*, and that hectic glittering in her spellbinding gaze.

God, she was perfect.

He never seemed to get enough of her.

Kane hooked his finger around the lace of her bra, pulling it down and dipping his head, letting his tongue trace tiny whorls around one proud, taut nipple. Round and round, in more and more intricate patterns, as Mattie—

his Mattie—made appreciative noises and arched her back all the more. He ran his hand down her spine, able to feel the fire building up inside her—the same one building inside him—and with every sweep of his tongue he kept on stoking it. Higher, and higher, and higher.

Only when she tunnelled her fingers through his hair, almost as if a part of her was afraid he might stop before she was ready, did he draw one perfect nipple into his mouth and suck. Hard.

Mattie cried out, a low and throaty sound that rumbled right through him, straight to his sex. So tight it was almost painful. *Almost.*

'Don't stop, Kane.'

It was little more than a whisper. A plea into the night. But he had no intention of stopping. He couldn't have anyway, even if he'd tried. Not when Mattie was encouraging him on with the roll of her hips and every arch of her back. So instead he shifted sides to lavish the same attention on her other breast. To elicit the same heady response.

Just as she'd always done. As though…as though she'd always been his.

The realisation walloped Kane with unexpected force.

Lust flashed through every inch of Mattie's body. Through a haze of desire it occurred to her that she wasn't far away from coming apart just from Kane's tongue on her breasts.

Surely she ought to be embarrassed at how easily she fell? But she wasn't. Not remotely. Still, there was no harm in retaking the reins a little, was there?

Wriggling on his lap, she pressed herself against him, solid and ready even through their trousers, making him groan. Making them both groan. And making her realise, far too late, that she wasn't in control of anything at all. Least of all her thundering heart.

When Kane moved his hands to her hips, lifting her

off him for a moment, she actually felt bereft. But then he flipped her around, laying her down until she was lying on her back on the bedroll, and after pulling off his tops with one economical movement he lowered his body to cover hers.

Hard, and ready, and full of deliciously uncompromising promise. Mattie sighed in appreciation and ran her hands over the sculpted ridges of his back. Then her fingernails. She dipped below his waistband to cup his backside and pull him against her as she shifted her legs until the hardest part of him was settled against the softest part of her.

Bliss.

'If you carry on like that, I can't guarantee this is going to last long once I'm inside you,' he growled, and she might have giggled at the seriousness of his expression had her body not been roaring for him to do exactly what he was saying.

She shifted again and felt him flex against her heat, his sharp intake of breath speaking louder than any words could. And the idea that Kane was almost as close to the edge as she was was just too thrilling.

Kane seemed to think so too. Because the next thing Mattie knew, he was lifting himself up from her, like the most elegant push-up she'd ever seen, before rolling back on his heels and reaching for her boots.

She watched transfixed as he swiftly removed first her remaining clothes then his, all the while the moonlight and firelight seeming to take it in turns to dance across his bronzed, hewn torso.

Kane Wheeler. The first boy she'd ever loved.

And the man a part of her would probably always love. No doubt there were a million reasons why this—here, now—was a bad idea, not least because they could have no future together. Not the way things stood. Yet Mattie couldn't bring herself to care.

She'd tried moving on and look where that had got her. Her career as a colonel and as a doctor were her future, and that would be more than enough. But tonight she had one more thing. She had Kane, the only man who had ever been able to tease her until she'd gone practically out of her mind with desire.

Funny how she should remember that suddenly.

'One more night,' she whispered, not knowing whether she was asking or telling.

'One more night,' he rasped back, but it told her nothing.

Then, before she could speak again, he lowered his head and drew one hard nipple into the wet heat of his mouth again, cupping her other breast with his big hand and flicking the pad of his thumb over the pink bud.

Mattie's mind went instantly blank. She gasped as sensations surged through her, turning her inside out all over again. Wicked tongue, clever tongue, and all Kane. She gave herself up to the exquisite torture as he worked his way across her body. Down her body.

And then he was right...*there.*

His shoulders were between her thighs, nudging her legs wider, and wider again, as though he wanted to take just a moment to savour the view. She could feel his breath warm on her sex and only making her ache for him all the more. All her senses were so heightened, so taut, like any of those fragile ties could snap at any moment, and yet she held still. Her fingers were tunnelled into Kane's hair but she forced herself to hold still, not to give in to this desperation.

And then he licked into her and white heat slammed through her. She bit her lip to keep from crying out, but she lifted her hips and rocked, unable to help herself, especially when he grasped her backside in his hands and held her in place. Gentle yet firm, reminding her that this was *his* show as he kept on playing with her hot, wet core.

Mattie could hardly stand it, and yet she couldn't get enough. She wanted more.

Needed more.

She could hear her own ragged breathing loud in the quiet night air but she didn't care. She was nearly mindless, hurtling towards some invisible edge, and still Kane kept driving her on. Letting his tongue slide over her, drawing lazy patterns on her before dipping inside. He knew exactly what to do to send her wild.

Only when she thought she couldn't take any more did he finally, *finally*, draw her into his mouth and suck, slipping a long finger deep inside her. Then another.

Mattie cried out, her hips bucking as she came apart, right there in a ruined building in the middle of nowhere, and still Kane didn't stop. She fractured and splintered as if wave after wave of spine-shattering intensity were tossing tiny parts of her into the ether, never to be recovered.

Mattie had no idea how long it took her to come back to herself. Minutes perhaps. Or maybe hours. But when she finally did, it was to the blissful sight of Kane, hard and intense, and the most masculine sight she'd ever seen in her life, moving up her body.

He drew her into his arms as he settled himself between her legs, nudging her with his sex and, incredibly, making her begin to ache already. Cupping his face, she met his searching gaze, almost believing that he was trying to see right into her soul. Right into her heart.

The thought was simultaneously thrilling and terrifying. Yet she held the contact, refusing to let her eyes drop away. And then he slid inside her, slowly at first, giving her chance to recover. She let her fingers drift down his jawline. Tight and locked and intense as if it was costing Kane dearly to keep the pace low. As though with one swivel of her hips she could send him hurtling off into the same oblivion he had just sent her.

She found she liked the idea.

He slid carefully inside her again and, without warning, Mattie twisted her body, drawing him in deeper. Faster. His low, almost feral grunt was wantonly satisfying.

'Be careful, Mattie,' he gritted out. 'My self-control is rapidly slipping.'

'I'm counting on it,' Mattie breathed, hooking her legs around his hips and pulling him in hard before locking them at his back.

A fresh wall of heat and need surged over her, as if she hadn't already come apart only a short while ago. She clung to him, helpless to stop her fingers from biting into the solid muscles of his arms, his back. But it was Kane, muttering darkly as he lost whatever remaining grip he'd had on his own senses and plunged into her, driving home, that really sent her spinning again. Shaking with the intensity of her hunger.

Then, *at last*, they were moving together. Riding the same waves of pleasure, faster and higher than ever before. And this time, when Mattie shattered into a thousand bright, tiny splinters, calling Kane's name as she broke apart, he followed her.

She was never going to be the same.

They were lying snuggled together in the double sleeping bag they had made by zipping their two bags together, and Mattie snuggled her back tighter into Kane's chest, wallowing in the feel of his arms wrapped tightly around her. His body was so hot against hers and she wanted to bask in that glow forever.

But they didn't have *forever*, did they?

How had she ever thought it would be different? Why had she pretended that she could control this...*thing* that had always arced between her and Kane? Had she ever really thought, deep down, that one more night would be enough?

As if it would *ever* be enough for her.

Because the simple truth was that she loved him. She always had and she always would. They just could never be together. There wasn't room in the army for both of them if they wanted to be together. But the worst of it was that she didn't even know if Kane felt the same way.

Was this one night—or these two nights, if she including the one back in Castleton—enough for him?

Mattie couldn't bring herself to ask. Instead, she stared into the dying flames of the fire in front of her, telling herself that wasn't an ominous sign.

For a moment Mattie faltered, uncertain what to say next. And then she began to speak before her brain even knew what she was saying.

'I told you that I thought I'd imagined seeing you at my wedding rehearsal, before I called off my engagement.'

'You did.' His tone was careful, and she didn't blame him. 'You also said you called off your engagement because marrying George Blakeney meant having to give up your army career.'

'Yes.' She moved her head slowly, still not turning. Still relishing the feel of his strong, capable body at her back. 'But also…because at that moment I realised that I *wanted* to have seen you.'

She felt rather than heard his sharp exhalation.

'Say again?'

'I wanted it to be you. I wanted you to have come for me. I think that's why Hayden called you, because a part of him knew that.'

'What are you telling me, Mattie? You never loved your fiancé?'

'No, I did. I did love George,' she began. 'In some way.

He was good, and kind, and caring. I knew we wouldn't be unhappy together. But I wasn't *in love* with him.'

'You looked like you loved him,' he managed tightly. Painfully. 'That night I watched you on that stage together.'

'I tried to, but...' She shook her head. 'Fourteen years and I've never moved on. I tried to, you know that, but I couldn't. You were always there, haunting my thoughts.'

'There's never been anyone else for me either,' Kane bit out almost harshly so that, for a moment, Mattie wasn't sure whether he felt that was a good thing or a bad one. 'But we can't be together like this. Both still serving.'

Silence swirled around them.

'I know,' she acknowledged eventually. 'But I can't leave. I almost made that mistake once before, but I know it would have been the wrong choice. I would have ended up resenting George. And I refuse to ever risk resenting you.'

The silence grew heavier. She was almost surprised with Kane broke it.

'Are you asking me to quit?'

Was she?

Mattie hesitated for a heartbeat before answering.

'No,' she told him firmly. 'I'm not asking that at all. I'm just...explaining why I can't leave my army career.'

'Neither can I.' His voice was hoarser than she expected. As though the words were painful for him to say.

In an odd way, that helped.

'I'd guessed as much,' she whispered, shifting onto her back so that could turn and finally face him.

The expression on his face was dark, making her stomach dip and roll.

'If I was going to leave for anyone, it would be you,' he told her fiercely, his hand tilting her chin up as he stared into her eyes in a way that made her heart actually ache. 'But I can't. I won't.'

Her whole world was beginning to crumble, like the

tide coming in to reclaim the castles they'd build on the beach as kids.

Yet she hadn't even realised her world had been made of sand.

'Kane, I never said—'

'This is my life, too,' he cut her off quietly. 'It might not have been my dream since birth, as it was for you, but the army has made me the man I am. It's who I am now.'

'You were always that man to me,' she told him. 'Even as kids. If you hadn't been, you never would have kept yourself away from the life that your father led. Or your brothers.'

She heard him wince, even if she didn't see it. Like she'd landed some blow she hadn't even been aware she was throwing.

'I didn't keep away from them, though. Not until it was too late anyway. You always thought I was so different from my brothers, and from my dad, but the truth is, before you came along, I was pretty much the same. I just wasn't as far down that path.'

'You're talking about this thing you did when you were a kid?'

He didn't answer, and she faltered for a moment then shrugged, as though it didn't matter. Though every fibre of her being was crying out for him to tell her. To finally let her in.

'You don't have to say anything more. Not if you don't want to.'

Still, she held her breath. Right up until he finally started to speak.

'The night it all happened I was with my brothers in a stolen car. They were wasted so I was driving.'

'You were fifteen,' she cried, unable to help herself even as she instantly regretted interrupting.

Kane watched her closely, a dark frown clouding his features and making her fingers long to smooth it away.

'Anyway, we stopped at an off licence. That Eight-Till-Late over on Beech Street, you remember? It was where my brothers always got their gear from.'

She remembered it. Some hole in the wall notorious for alcoholics, and the night staff selling illicit drugs.

'Only when we got there, they weren't buying anything. They both had guns, goodness knows where they got them from, and I realised they were holding up the place. Worse, I was their getaway driver.'

She sucked in a shocked breath.

'Tell me you called the police, Kane. Tell me you drove off and called 999.'

He raked his hand through his hair, and she could *feel* his despair and regret.

'I should have. Of course I should have. But… I didn't think the police would believe me.'

She opened her mouth to argue then closed it again.

She remembered only too well what Kane's experience of the police had been back then. The Wheeler clan had been hated and feared in equal measure. If something went wrong in Heathdale, from house invasions to drunken brawls, from the cobblestone set on the dock road being taken up to the copper on the church roof disappearing, the Wheeler clan had likely been involved. People—everyone—had been desperate to get rid of them. All of them. And Kane was a Wheeler.

Still…

'You waited for them, didn't you, and then you drove them home? Or wherever they were going.'

'I didn't know what else to do, Matz. I was fifteen and I was in shock. I knew they were bad but even I had no idea what they were capable of.'

'And afterwards, when the shock wore off?'

She hated the bleak look that clouded his dark eyes. *Hated* it.

'I ditched the car and I went home. I expected the police to show up on the doorstep any minute. I was ready to confess everything, and I was ready to take whatever punishment I was given. But one hour turned into two, then twelve. Then a day, a week, a month. So I stayed quiet. But from then on I tried to keep my distance. I told them to leave me out of whatever they did next, or I'd turn them in. I never let myself get dragged into anything with them ever again.'

'My God, Kane.'

'That was also when I got myself a motorbike. I figured I couldn't be tied to them if people always saw me around town on that thing.'

'I remember it.' Her body flushed in spite of everything. It had been a few more years until they'd started dating, but the number of times she'd been on the back of that bike. The delicious *things* she and Kane had done on it. 'Why didn't you ever tell me?'

He shook his head.

'Why would I risk losing you? You were the first person who had ever treated me with anything other than contempt. You told me that I wasn't like them, and that I was better than anything my life had to offer. I couldn't stand to see the look in your eyes when you realised that you were wrong.'

'I would never have thought that!' she exclaimed. 'I would have believed you and I would have helped you.'

'Would you, though? Really?' Kane challenged. 'You knew my family's reputation. Would you really have been that quick to trust me over anyone else if you had known?'

She opened her mouth to argue, then closed it again. As much as she balked at admitting it, maybe he was right.

'You changed me, Matz. *You.* And your family showed me there was a different way. A better way.'

'So what happened?' she asked at last. 'How did you end up leaving that night?'

She was afraid to hear, but afraid not to. It was impossible to shake the feeling that his story was leading somewhere she didn't understand. And yet the urge to finally understand the truth, after all these years, was sharp and driving.

'In the end, my past caught up with me.' Kane twisted his mouth into something that was more bared teeth than any kind of smile. 'I was heading home after being with you when the police came for my brothers. They'd held up another off licence, but this one had CCTV.'

'The police identified them?'

'They had a hunch but no clear identification. Still, I saw the lights, heard the commotion, as I was about to turn into the street, so I just kept going. I didn't stop. But I figured it was only a matter of time before the police put the two crimes together and came for me. I couldn't think of any way out. So... I rode straight back to your house.'

'You came to my dad.' She froze, her brain desperately trying to make sense of it all, piecing the puzzle together slowly.

Yet at least now she actually *had* the pieces.

'I came to see you. To apologise.'

'Why?' she whispered.

He paused.

'Because you were the only one who ever believed in me, and I had betrayed your trust.'

It was too much, and at the same time not enough. She wished she could go back and change it all. Though whether for Kane or for herself, she couldn't be certain. Possibly both.

'You never found me,' she finally managed.

'No. Your dad caught me about to try to shimmy up that drainpipe at the back of your house. He demanded to know what the hell I thought I was doing, and I'm not sure if he wasn't about to kick me into next week, but I ended up telling him everything.'

'He never said.'

Not in fourteen years. And yet, if she was to understand it now, he'd tasked Hayden with contacting Kane in the run up to her wedding to another man.

'He went straight to some high-ranking police chief he knew, and they made a deal that as long as I made a statement testifying against my brothers, they would never prosecute me. To this day I don't know how long I was with them, answering their questions. Then your father put me in a car with some old army buddy of his who drove me to the army barracks where I signed up on the spot. He called it my one chance for a fresh start.'

'I just can't… It's so…' She stopped.

Her whole world was spinning sideways, and she had no way to stop it. For over a decade she'd believed that Kane had walked away from her. She'd even considered that her father had offered him money to leave, though a part of her had never quite been able to believe it. Not of either of them.

But she'd never contemplated that Kane hadn't had much of a choice. Or that her own father had played such a part in getting rid of the boy she had loved.

'It was the best thing he could have done for me, Matz.' Kane's voice tugged her back to the present, reading her mind. 'I was able to reinvent myself in a way I never could have done anywhere else.'

'You could have—'

'No, I couldn't have. I owe your father so much. I like who I am now. I like what the army made me. I owe them.

And that's why I can't leave. Becoming some security firm guy—for the money—isn't the way to repay anyone. It doesn't make me proud.'

Mattie clenched her arms around Kane's, wanting to respond but not knowing where to start. None of this was what she wanted to hear, yet the hardest part about it was that she understood exactly what was driving him.

She was even proud of him for it. And proud of her father for being there for Kane when no one else had been.

But in some ways that also made it that much worse.

'So we're back to square one?' she managed at last, her voice flat and emotionless. 'Fighting this chemistry yet unable to be together. *That* isn't what I want either.'

It felt like losing him all over again, only this time it was worse, because this time it came down to their choices.

'It can't be both, Matz. I'll leave in the morning. We did our job, we decided on new scenarios and it looks as though we've found the perfect location. Once we get back to the hospital in the morning, I'll write my notes up and take them to my CO.'

Something moved through Mattie. Swift and certain. They had made their choices, as impossible as they were. And they were for the right reasons. She and Kane ought to be proud that they'd allowed logic to prevail over emotion.

She could cry about it or she could make the most of the rest of this one opportunity. The words were out before she could second-guess herself.

'We still have the rest of tonight.'

'We do,' he agreed slowly.

'After this you'll be going back to your infantry company. We'll never see each other again.'

'We won't,' he growled, the roughness of it rolling right through her.

'Then brace yourself, Kane.' She lifted her hands to his jaw and held it fiercely. 'It's going to be a long, sleepless night.'

CHAPTER TWELVE

'MATTIE, CAN YOU join the MERT team?'

Mattie's head snapped up from her desk as her second-in-command burst through her office door with barely a knock. She was writing up her own notes and pretending that she wasn't nursing an aching heart since Kane had left camp a couple of hours earlier.

But now she was up on her feet before she'd even replied.

'What is it, Kath?'

'Emergency call just came through on the field phone. Infantry soldier, penetrating chest wound, possible thoracotomy, and Clark is already in Theatre. You're the next best choice.'

Wordlessly, Mattie rounded her desk and raced down the corridor with Kath to the HEMS area, knowing every precious second counted. Such severe injuries on exercise weren't common, but this was a live firing exercise and so accidents weren't unheard of.

As a specialist cardiothoracic surgeon, Clark was the go-to guy for this, which was why they had tried to incorporate this training into some of the exercises recently. But this wasn't one of her scenarios. This was a real-life trauma, and if a thoracotomy was going to be performed in the back of the helicopter and Clark wasn't available, she was the best person to do it. She had been on more tours and had more experience than anyone else here.

'Cole, Nilson, Jones, with me,' she commanded, grabbing her gear and heading to the door.

There would be a full thoracotomy pack on board, but she grabbed an emergency serrated wire, clamps, scalpel and heavy scissors.

They had minutes to get their kit on, helmets, body armour, pelvic protection, knee pads, and to sprint to the helicopter with their gear. But it was a drill Mattie knew well, and all too quickly the chopper was dipping as it sped through the skies, reached the zone and landed.

At least with an exercise things could be halted, which meant that if surgical intervention was necessary she would be able to do it on the ground, and not in the back of the chopper whilst it was on the flight back.

If the injured soldier hadn't gone into cardiac arrest she would keep him stable on the flight back. But if he had, the maximum time for surgical intervention following the loss of cardiac output would be ten minutes. And the flight out would take up a hefty chunk of that.

She just had to fight off any paralyzing thoughts that the infantry soldier she was flying out to try to save could, so easily, be Kane.

By the time the helicopter landed and Mattie's team was leaping off the back, the combat medics already had the injured soldier intubated and were ventilating him. And it wasn't Kane.

This time, a tiny voice needled.

'Get full IV access and get him into a supine position,' she ordered her team.

A rapid application of skin prep would have to do—there wasn't time for full asepsis. Taking the scalpel and forceps, she felt for the fifth intercostal space and made a series of deep midline lateral incisions, then waited. If tension pneumothorax decreased, and cardiac output returned, she wouldn't continue with the procedure.

There was no change. *Dammit.*

'Okay, let's push on. Scissors.'

Nilson handed her the scissors and Mattie connected the thoracostomies, then she inserted two fingers to hold the lung safely out the way whilst she cut through the all the layers of intercostal muscles and pleura, leaving only a narrow sternal bridge between the anterolateral thoracotomies.

'Saw,' she demanded. The scissors were taken from her and the serrated wire placed into her hand instead.

Time to cut through the sternum.

She worked as quickly as she could, cutting with long, smooth strokes from the inside out. There would be retractors in the full thoracotomy pack but there was no time for that.

'Grab here…' she indicated to Cole '…and open up the chest cavity as far as you can. I need access. Scissors.'

Then, tenting the pericardium to minimise the risk to the nerves that ran through the lateral walls of the pericardial sac, Mattie made a longer midline longitudinal cut with the scissors, evacuated the blood and clot and began inspecting the heart for the site of the bleeding.

Her hope was that the heart would spontaneously restart, with a return of full cardiac output. Her fear was that it would remain in asystole. She held her breath and continued her rapid but systematic inspection.

And then the heart flickered. Began to pump again. Slowly. *Too slowly.*

'We have a heartbeat,' someone—Cole possibly—exclaimed.

Mattie shook her head,

'Reduced output. We need to find the wounds and close

them, then try massaging the heart. Wait… I think I see the hole.'

It was small. *Thank God.*

'Here.' Grabbing Nilson's hand, she pulled it into the soldier's chest. 'Plug your finger right…*there.* Good. Now, don't move it. Jones, get ready with the anaesthesia. If the procedure is successful, he's going to start to wake up.'

Slipping her hands around the heart, one on the posterior surface and the other on the anterior, Mattie began to massage from the apex upwards whilst ensuring she kept the heart horizontal. All the while she counted under her breath, trying to achieve optimal beats per minute of around eighty.

And then she felt the heart begin to take over, beating harder, faster. A return to full cardiac output—along with more bleeding.

'Don't move your finger.' She looked grimly at Nilson. 'We're going to need to get him back to the field hospital for surgery and a full repair. It's down to you to keep that hole in his heart plugged until we get there.'

And the moment Operation Strikethrough was over she was going to head back to the UK to see her father. If she could catch him on a good day—though they were rarer now—maybe she could ask him about Kane and see what he had to say.

Because if today had taught her anything, it was that it was true what they said—life really was simply too short.

'He's worse than I last time I was here, Hayd.' Mattie held onto the kitchen doorframe, her back to her brother as he prepared fresh tea for their father.

'I know,' Hayden replied grimly. 'I wish it hadn't been so long but…'

It hung there between them, unspoken. Between tours of duty, exercises away and compulsory courses there was no possible way that they could see their father more frequently. It was why they had employed a live-in carer, not just so that they knew he was being looked after but also because it provided him with the company and stimulation he needed. As well as allowing him to remain in his home where everything felt familiar to him. Safe.

The military was the life they had chosen, just as it had been the life that he had chosen. Still, it didn't entirely diminish the guilt.

'He keeps thinking I'm Mum.'

'He keeps thinking I'm his buddy from the Falklands.' Hayden arched his eyebrows and Mattie laughed, some of her sadness receding for a moment. 'There's no point trying to correct him, Mattie. If it gives him some pleasure, why not just leave him?'

'I know, I just…' She wrinkled her nose. 'At least with you, you're getting all the secret stories he never he told us over the years.'

'True. Some of them are shocking, even to me. Dammit, we're out of milk.'

'Vera will be back in an hour with the shopping. No doubt she'll bring some in.'

They'd both offered to do it for her, but the older woman had tutted them away and told Mattie that they were here to visit the Brigadier and not to do errands for her. It had surprised them both when she'd also told them that their father usually liked to accompany her to the shops, taking his time to potter up and down the aisles, even if he couldn't remember what they were doing there.

'I'll nip to the corner shop, if you're okay with Dad?'

'Of course.' Pushing herself off the doorframe, Mattie plastered a bright smile on her lips and smoothed her jumper, which was in her mother's favourite colour. No wonder her father was getting confused.

She strode confidently back into the living room.

'Hey. Dad, Hayd is just going out for milk for our tea.'

'Hayden?' Her father lifted his head from his paper to frown at her. 'Mary, darling, he's at university—how can he go to the shop?'

'It's Mattie, Dad. Your daughter. Not Mum… Mary.'

'Mathilda?' His peered at her harder, before covering smoothly. 'Of course. I was just miles away. How have you been?'

'I've been well, Dad.' Mattie smiled, relieved he had recognised her. Sometimes he didn't realise even when she told him. Soon it wouldn't matter what she said.

'Another tour?'

'There's a plan for a new army battalion,' she told him, even though she knew he wouldn't remember. 'I was running the medical support arm, seeing if the new strategies would hold up.'

'I remember testing a new strike plan back in 1992, or was it 1993? In between operational tours.' He smiled a soft, almost haunting smile. He was sinking back into his memories already. 'Operation Strongarm, we called it.'

'This was Operation Strikethrough,' she told him, trying to pull him back to the present even though she couldn't have said why. And then another thought hit her. 'I saw Kane.'

'Kane?'

'You remember.' She flicked out her tongue to wet her lips. 'Kane Wheeler? I never realised he had joined up all those years ago.'

Her father stared out of the window, blinking slowly. Mattie had no idea she'd held her breath until he suddenly spoke again.

'What are we going to tell Mathilda about the Wheeler boy, Mary?'

Mattie opened her mouth then closed it.

'What about Kane?' she asked cautiously. Hating herself.

'He's gone, Mary. And we're going to have to be the people to tell her. It's going to crush her.'

'What did you do?' she asked carefully. Not certain that she should be doing it but unable to help herself.

She had Kane's side of the story, but she still needed to know—to understand—what her father had thought all those years ago.

Why he'd never told her the truth.

'I had to help him, Mary,' her father said firmly. 'Mathilda won't see it that way, of course, but that can't be helped. There was no other way. That young Wheeler boy doesn't deserve to get pulled down by the rest of his abominable family.'

'Where did he go?' Mattie could barely recognise her own voice. She had no idea how she managed to sound so calm, so collected.

'It's best you don't know, Mary. It's best that no one knows. He's given the police enough to send those brothers of his away for a decent length of time. So neither they nor that father of theirs can find out where Kane is. They would hunt the kid down and they make him pay.'

Mattie blinked. It almost sounded as though her father was protective of Kane, yet all these years she'd thought her parents had hated him.

How could she have been so wrong?

Her heart felt as though it was about to beat right out of her chest.

'Surely he could have said goodbye to…Mathilda.' She faltered for a moment.

Her father snorted, though there was still tenderness in his voice. 'Don't be foolish, Mary—do you think our little Mathilda would have left it at that? She'd have inveigled the whole story out of him—you know that Wheeler boy would do anything for her—and our daughter is nothing if not hot-headed.'

A proud smile touched his lips now, despite everything.

'She would no doubt march up to the Wheelers' house and give the lot of them a piece of her mind. But those boys are both facing jail sentences so how safe do you think she would be, Mary? As it stands, they have no idea where Kane is now, or that I had anything to do with it. This way both the boy, and our family, are guaranteed to stay safe.'

Mattie started, then went cold. When Kane had told her, he'd deliberately left out the more sordid facts. The danger he'd been in.

Plus, her father was right, she *had* had a tendency to act before thinking back then, and Kane's brothers had never been the most rational, predictable of boys, and both had racked up a long list of violent offences, as far as she was aware. She could have caused no end of trouble not just for herself but for her whole family if she'd gone off at the deep end on them.

'Besides, he asked me not to say anything to her.'

Mattie turned back, watching her father carefully.

'Who asked you not to say anything?'

'The Wheeler lad, of course.' He clicked his tongue impatiently.

'Why not?' she pressed, reining in her impatience when he didn't elaborate.

Her father pulled his eyebrows together, the slight shake of his head almost imperceptible. 'Shame, I imagine, Mary. He didn't want Mathilda to know. I suppose he thought it would change the way she looked at him. Taint it slightly. He'd always been the only one in that dreadful family to stay out of trouble with the police. I think he wanted to preserve that image she had of him, rather than know the truth.'

Mattie stared. She could practically feel the cogs spinning and slipping in her head. She probably wouldn't have understood at the time, but in hindsight it made sense that

Kane might want to hide the truth from her. But her father? All these years she'd thought her father hated Kane. She'd imagined that he'd have taken any opportunity to convince her that her first boyfriend hadn't been worthy of her.

Instead, the truth was that her father had protected the one secret Kane hadn't wanted her to know. And she loved them both for it.

'Is there anything else?' she pressed quietly, but her father had switched back to staring out of the window and she knew he was lost in his own thoughts, leaving her to try to pick her way through the unexpected bombshell.

She was still musing when her brother walked back in with the milk and a huge round box of chocolates in his hand.

'Who are they for?' She forced a laugh, grateful for the distraction. 'Dad, or you?'

'Their Dad's favourite.' Hayden, oblivious to the turmoil in her head, at least had the grace to look sheepish as she followed him into the kitchen and dropped them on the island.

'But you quite fancied them?' Mattie lifted her eyebrows.

He lifted his hands, palms up.

'I admit nothing.'

She sank into a chair and toyed with the plastic seal on the box as he set about making fresh tea. It was only when she heard her brother clicking his fingers by her ear that she realised he'd been talking to her and she hadn't heard a word.

'Sorry, what?' Sitting up straighter, she affected levity.

She might have known Hayden wouldn't be fooled.

'What's happened, Mattie?'

'Nothing.'

'Mattie,' he chastised, but then turned his back as though concentrating on the hot drinks.

Knowing that would somehow make it easier to talk.

'Dad thought I was Mum again.' She stopped. Waited. But Hayden didn't press her, leaving her to continue in her own time. 'Did you know he helped Kane to leave because his brothers had held up that Eight-Till-Late in town?'

Her brother didn't answer immediately, but eventually he half glanced back, his head over his shoulder.

'Dad helped Kane leave because he gave evidence against his brothers.'

Whatever she had expected, it wasn't that. She tried to process the information, but her head was spinning hard. Beginning to pound. Another thought walloped her.

'You knew? Wait, is that why you invited Kane to London? To my wedding rehearsal?'

She heard silence as he stopped stirring the tea. Then the clink as he set the spoon down. Finally, Hayden turned around.

'I contacted Kane because Dad asked me to.'

'Dad did?' She kept her voice low because as much as shouting wasn't her, right now she wanted to yell and roar, and probably beat her bloody hands on her chest. 'What did he say?'

Hayden folded his arms over his chest.

'Not much. He was already into the illness by then, you know that.'

The pounding in her head grew louder, like a marching band made up of every drummer in the entire military.

'He must have told you something.'

Her brother met her gaze head on.

'He contacted me out of the blue a few weeks before your wedding. Told me Kane was in the military and that I should contact an old army buddy of his from way back. He wanted me to tell Kane that you were getting married.'

'And?' she prompted.

'And about what happened that night with Kane and his brothers. But that was pretty much all he said.'

Mattie shook her head in disbelief.

'He must have told you more than that.'

'I shouldn't need to remind you how closed Dad could be, Mattie.'

She knew. But, still, it didn't entirely make sense.

'And you did it? Just like that? No questions asked?' She recognised that expression. Knew that lock of his jaw. 'What aren't you saying, Hayd?'

He still didn't answer.

'Please?'

He eyed her a little longer, still not speaking.

'I don't know, Mattie.' Hayden shook his head eventually. 'Dad was never exactly clear, but I got the impression that he wanted to make amends. And…maybe he thought that you didn't really love George.'

'And you didn't think to *tell* me?' Her voice rose an octave, and she had to fight to bring it back down. 'To pass on this information.'

'I thought about a million things,' Hayden declared at length. 'You were getting married, Mattie. To a guy who seemed perfect for you and who you said you loved. I didn't want to rake up the past at what was supposed to be such a happy time for you. Plus, I didn't know how much of what Dad said was accurate and how much was the Alzheimer's playing tricks.'

He had a point. A part of her could see that, even with her head whirling like she was some kind of mad, spinning-top ride.

'But what about afterwards?'

'Afterwards?'

She didn't mean to cluck her tongue.

'After George and I called it off?' she pressed irritably. 'After Kane had come up that night?'

'How was I to know that you hadn't spoken to him, Mattie?' Hayden shrugged. 'When you didn't say anything, I assumed you just didn't want to talk about it.'

She balled her hands into fists, trying to slow her racing mind. And heart. Yet slowly, *slowly*, even now, certain things were coming into focus.

'I didn't speak to him. I didn't even realise he had really been there. I thought I'd…conjured him up in my head or something. Until I saw him at Operation Strikethrough and he told me about being there that night.'

'You saw him? Out on exercise?'

'Yeah. He's a WO2. Percy Copperhead's CSM.'

'Ah.'

There was so much sentiment loaded into that one syllable that it lifted the tiny, fine hairs on the back of her neck.

'*Ah*, what?'

'*Ah*, so that's why you've been in such a weird mood ever since you got back.'

She opened her mouth to deny it but then snapped it shut. This was Hayd. What was the point in lying to him?

'You still should have asked me about him at my wedding rehearsal,' she said instead.

He leaned against the surface, arms across his chest, assessing her carefully.

'Maybe,' he conceded at last. 'But ultimately what difference would it have made? Would you be with Kane now if I had said anything?'

'How would I know that?'

'Okay, then answer this. Now you've met him again, what's changed? Clearly you can't both stay in and still be together, so are you leaving your career? Or is Kane leaving his?'

'Are you suggesting I should?' she snapped. 'Weren't you the one person who told me—repeatedly—that I was crazy for getting ready to give up my army career for George. But you think it's okay to give it up for Kane?'

'No, I didn't say that.' He arched his eyebrows at her. 'I used to think it was crazy to give up something you love for anyone else but yourself.'

'Used to?' She frowned and despite all the rowdiness inside her head, she couldn't help picking up on such an un-Hayden-like comment.

'Oh, no, this isn't about me right now.' He refused to be baited. 'This is about you. And my point is that you can blame Dad and me as much as you like for not telling you the truth back then, but this is now. You've had a chance to put things right *if* that's what you really want. But if you're both choosing your careers then that's on you two, Mattie. No one else.'

Then, turning around, he picked up her mug of tea and passed it to her. She cupped it in her hands and slid her fingers through the handle.

Mattie still glowered at her unconcerned brother over the rim, changing the subject as though it could somehow resolve the issues tumbling around her head.

'So, what's your next task anyway?'

'I'm supposed to be DS for a training exercise on Salisbury Plain.'

'Supposed to be?'

Another uncharacteristically Hayden comment but as he answered her, Mattie found herself losing focus, her head was still echoing with his earlier words.

He'd made a good point. She *did* have a chance to put things right if she really wanted to.

The question was, what *was* she prepared to do about it?

CHAPTER THIRTEEN

'MORNING, WILLIAM,' MATTIE greeted the adjutant, after checking the room to ensure he was alone.

'Hey, Mattie.' William stood up from his paperwork to step around his desk and greet her. 'How are things? Congratulations on your promotion, by the way. I hear it's going to be officially announced any day now. Especially after Operation Strikethrough was such a success, in no small part down to the work you and WO2 Wheeler put in.'

'Thanks,' she croaked out, plastering a bright smile to her lips, and told herself that William couldn't possibly know that she was about to resign her commission.

In fact, getting the call from William that the colonel wanted to see her couldn't have come at a more opportune moment.

She had been wrestling with the situation ever since her conversation with her brother. Two weeks of going back and forth, listening to her head and then her heart. It had consumed her every moment. She had barely eaten, barely slept, only work had provided some relief from her buffeting emotions.

When she'd been ready to resign her commission for George it had been because it was what had been expected of her as the new Lady Blakeney, and she'd ignored the niggling doubt that it would breed resentment in her marriage.

So surely it was foolish to be considering giving up her army career for Kane? Only her heart was telling her otherwise. It was reminding her that she would still have a great career as a civilian doctor. And what about when—if—she and Kane had children? She had always imagined herself as a doctor and a mother. But she'd never imagined herself as an army doctor and a mother. Much as she loved her father, she could remember all too clearly how much of her childhood, and Hayden's, he'd missed when he'd been away on exercise, or training camps, or courses.

It wasn't something she wanted for herself.

And then there was the fact that Kane had never once asked her to leave. They had never even discussed any real future together because it had seemed like an impossibility. All the same, she'd known her heart had been winning the debate. In fourteen years she hadn't moved on because of one simple truth: she was in love with Kane and she always had been.

Nothing had ever changed that. So if she didn't put herself out there and take that bold step, somehow, deep down, she knew she would regret it for the rest of her life. And if he rejected her then at least she would finally have closure.

Surely that was worth something?

'Mathilda.' The colonel's voice broke through the room, cutting William off as he was about to speak again.

'Colonel.' She braced slightly but he gestured for her to stop and go through to his office.

'Schedule's a bit tight today and the call I received from Major Copperhead of the new infantry force rather caught me off guard.'

Percy Copperhead? Kane's OC? What could *he* want?

'Before you start, sir,' Mattie began, 'I wonder if I might say something?'

'One moment, Mathilda.' The colonel halted her as he sat down. 'Come in and close the doors, please, William.'

He sat down as his adjutant closed the doors between the two offices, then gestured for Mattie to also sit and, with William also in the room, she found she didn't want to say anything she'd come to say after all.

'Everything you and WO2 Wheeler pulled off during that pre-phase of Operation Strikethrough was quite impressive. My counterpart from Infantry said that medical support kept the pressure on, and it really helped to test the new tactical battle group to its limits. Outstanding work.'

'Oh. Well. Good.'

She wanted to feel relieved, but she couldn't. Her resignation was rolling all around her mouth.

'This is rather a delicate part.' The CO steepled his fingers. 'It's about how well you know WO2 Wheeler.'

Mattie's stomach dipped and tumbled in an instant. She hadn't been prepared for this. She and Kane had been so discreet, how could anyone possibly have known what had happened between them? This certainly wasn't how she'd wanted to go out—under some cloud—but if it was going to happen then at least she knew it was for the right person.

It wasn't like it had been with George, because Kane had never been Blakeney. She would always have gone to the ends of the earth for Kane. And she knew she wouldn't live to regret a single moment of it.

'You want to know how well I know WO2 Wheeler?' She unglued her tongue from the roof of her mouth.

'This is all in strictest confidence, Major Brigham.' Her colonel reverted to her rank for a moment, as if to impress upon her the gravity of the situation. 'But Division have been considering WO2 Wheeler for LE in the next year or so, having been put forward by his previous commanding officer.'

Mattie's brain skidded, the smell of burning rubber filling her head.

Kane was being considered as an LE? Mattie paused, somewhere between being shocked and not being surprised at all. An LE—Late Entry Officer—was one of few soldiers who jumped the non-commissioned officer and commissioned officer divide. Usually only a very select number of Warrant Officers First Class were considered for the role.

He would be commissioned into the army as a captain, able to either take up a staff officer role or to serve as a CSM and WO1. More importantly, as a captain it would mean that she and Kane would be commissioned officers together. They could both remain in the army whilst any personal relationship between them would be entirely acceptable.

It was like Fate was somehow spinning everything perfectly together.

'That doesn't surprise me at all.' She had no idea how she managed to sound so controlled. 'WO2 Wheeler was easy to work with. Extremely knowledgeable and efficient. He would make an exceptional officer, in my opinion.'

The best part about it was that it was completely true.

'And mine,' her CO concurred. 'However, it seems Major Copperhead doesn't agree. Ever since he took over from the previous CO, he has been trying to quash WO2 Wheeler's recommendation.'

A thousand thoughts skittered through her head, but she couldn't voice a single one of them. They were too personal, too revealing. In the end she settled for a pointed, 'I think that's a mistake.'

'I agree. And so, it would seem, does Division. They would like to bring WO2 Wheeler's consideration forward.'

'Bring it forward?' she hedged, not even feigning disinterest.

'Forward to this year. Percy isn't happy about it, of course, but it's gone over his head. They asked me if I would like to second the recommendation, which I do.' He glared at her, as though she was going to argue. 'I rather hoped your recent experience working with him would help me to do that.'

For the briefest of moments Mattie couldn't answer. Kane was exactly the type of officer the army needed—far more than any of the Percy Copperheads. From where Kane had started, he was exactly the kind of role model the soldiers needed, and his experience would make him a knowledgeable but fair leader.

Something moved inside her chest. Happiness. And pride.

'Yes, sir, of course I can do that.'

'Good.' He looked satisfied. 'I'd like a report on my desk by this afternoon. Mattie, for our eyes only, please?'

'Understood.' She dipped her head, a thousand thoughts crowding inside it.

'In fact, Kane's been earmarked as the next Army Sergeant Major,' William confided unexpectedly, at some unseen gesture from the CO.

'Say again?'

It was more than Mattie could believe. The most senior member of the other ranks in the British Army, the post had only been created in a few years before, and both previous appointment holders had been former WO1s, later commissioned as captains.

Kane would be the newest holder. And Mattie couldn't think of a more deserving individual.

'That's…phenomenal,' she managed, a wave of nostalgia walloping her suddenly.

What she wouldn't have given to be able to tell her father that the kindness he'd shown Kane all those years ago hadn't been wasted. He would have been so proud.

She was only sorry that it had taken her until now to know it.

Kane removed his headwear as he stepped through the doors to his battalion headquarters, as protocol dictated, and made his way up the long, winding stairs to his adjutant's office to get an appointment with his CO.

No doubt relaying his decision to Percy Copperhead would give the guy the kick of the year, but Kane told himself he didn't care. He'd spent too many weeks without Mattie, and he'd hated it.

Dedicating himself to his army career had been one thing fourteen years ago. But now, after those nights they'd spent together—and all those revelations—his career had lost some of its lustre. At least, when compared to what he had with her.

If he could have had both, it would have been perfect, but having to choose made it a no-brainer. He would have been to see his CO earlier, if the guy hadn't sent him to run yet another needless training course, as if to take up as much of his downtime as possible.

The guy wasn't to know that Kane had welcomed every moment of it. It had kept his mind busy whilst he'd tried to grapple with the gravity of giving up his entire career for the woman he loved—with the risk that she might not even want him.

But it didn't matter, he had to try. He would never forgive himself if he didn't.

Mattie had been right, back in that ruin the last night they'd been together. He had more prospects now than he'd had had as a kid. People head-hunting him. He would earn more money to provide for his family. He had something to offer her. Which was why it wasn't the impossible decision he'd feared it would be, to walk away from it all for her.

The last thing he anticipated, when he reached the top of the staircase, was to see Mattie leaving Copperhead's office, a grim expression on her face.

Everything fell away and in that split second there was no army, no building. Only her, and him. Something bubbled inside him at the mouth-watering sight of her walking down the corridor, every step a picture in elegance and barely restrained anger.

'Mat... Major,' he growled, changing his term of address at the last moment.

She stopped abruptly, her head snapping up to look at him, and Kane had to draw in a steadying breath, scarcely able to believe how much self-control it was taking him not to simply stride over and take her in his arms.

But there were too many people around and, as far as they were concerned, she was a major and he was a warrant officer.

'Hello, ma'am, what brings you here?'

'Mr Wheeler.' She inclined her head politely, her eyes taking in everyone around them without appearing to be looking anywhere. 'A little bit of final business on Operation Strikethrough.'

She was lying. He couldn't read the look that danced over her lovely features, but he knew there was something going on.

'Actually, it's fortuitous that I've seen you. Do you have five minutes?'

Only he could know her well enough to hear the shake of anticipation in her voice. Was the same buzzing thrill zipping madly around her body at this very moment, the way it was his?

He'd really wanted to speak to Copperhead before he

spoke to Mattie, but there was no way he could refuse her. No way he wanted to.

'Certainly,' he acquiesced. 'Which way?'

'This is your battalion HQ, Mr Wheeler, I wonder if you would lead the way.'

Wordlessly, he led her along the corridor to one of the quieter training rooms, set up a little like a classroom. He opened the door for her then followed her inside.

She moved around the other side of the desks and looked at him.

'So what *are* you doing here, Matz?' he asked quietly. 'And don't flannel me with final reports on Operation Strikethrough.'

'I can't tell you.' There was the vaguest hint of anguish in her tone, making him believe her, before she turned the question back on him. 'What are *you* doing here, Kane?'

'Me? Oh, I've come to buy myself out.'

He rather liked it that her mouth actually fell open a little. Though the urge to close it by claiming it with his own was incredibly powerful.

'You're leaving?' she breathed.

'That's the idea.'

He didn't miss the way she reached out, clutching the table beside herself, almost as if she needed the solid surface to keep herself from stumbling.

He liked it that he had that effect on her. *Still.*

'Why?' she choked out after a few moments.

'Why do you think, Matz? It's the only way we can be together.'

'No.' She began to shake her head. *'No!'*

This wasn't quite what he'd had in mind.

'Why not? That's what I want—to be with you. I should have seen it before, but the fact is that I've seen it now.'

'No, Kane, you can't do that.' And this time there was no hesitation in her tone.

A heavy beat started up in his chest, echoing through his head. He pretended he didn't hear it.

'That isn't quite the reaction I was hoping for, Matz.'

'I don't want you to leave.'

'Well, I want to.'

'For me?'

'For *us*.'

Again she shook her head, and Kane found himself grinding his teeth.

'I don't want to play this game, Matz. We love each other, we both said it. But neither of us were prepared to give up our careers for the other. Only now I *am* prepared to. Because after all that's happened between us, I realise that this career means nothing if I don't have you.'

'I still can't let you buy yourself out,' she gritted out.

He pushed off from the desk, taking a step closer to her, that fresh, citrusy fragrance pervading his senses, and that fire in her eyes stoking the flames that burned inside him.

'I want to be with you, Mattie. I thought the army was the most important thing to me, and perhaps it was. But only because it was the only thing that filled the void that had opened up when I lost you.'

'You're saying you would choose me over the career that you love?' she asked breathlessly, finding that her soul ached to hear the words.

'I would. And I am,' he told her simply. 'But I know you, Mathilda Brigham. This isn't your cue to start feeling guilty because you don't want to quit too. That isn't what it's about.'

'I won't,' she replied promptly, but there was a teasing quality to her tone that made him take stock.

'Am I missing something?'

'You might be.'

Okay, now she was definitely teasing him. Tentatively, given where they were, but it was there.

He studied her more intently.

'What's going on, Matz?'

It was there, bursting to get out of her. He could read it in every exquisite line of her body. And how he wanted to press that body to his again.

'I already went to my CO to resign my commission to be with you.'

Of all the things he'd considered she could have said, that wasn't one of them.

'Say again?' He heard the anger threaded through his tone before he felt it.

'I decided the same thing that you have. That I wasn't willing to sacrifice a relationship with you for a career in the army. Not when I could still do the thing I really love—being a doctor—in the civilian world.'

'You love being an *army* doctor, though,' he ground out.

'I do. And you love being an infantry man.'

'Not as much as I love you.'

She faltered. He saw it. She almost circled the desk back to him but caught herself, and Kane was glad. He wasn't sure he'd have had the self-control to resist if she'd done that.

'So…you really quit?' he demanded. And it didn't make him anywhere near happy. 'You can't. I don't ever want you to grow to resent me because you lost the career you love.'

'I wouldn't have. As much as I love being an army doctor, I know people are what matter more. *You* matter more.'

'No, Mattie, I won't accept that.'

'Well, we can debate that another time, but look at it this way instead. In the end I didn't resign.'

For the second time is as many moments he felt winded. So she *had* loved him enough to leave but had then changed her mind?

'You don't know why your CO has called you, do you?' she asked with a soft laugh.

'I don't care,' he told her, his expression intense and serious, making her sober instantly.

'You should,' she chastised him. 'And I shouldn't tell you this, but I don't want you to blow it by asking to buy yourself out. You know Percy will jump at the chance, and then everything everyone else is doing will be for nothing.'

He shouldn't be curious, yet he was.

'What do you mean, *everything everyone else is doing*?'

'I mean, your former CO put you forward for a recommendation as an LE. And my CO, following my report on our working relationship during Operation Strikethrough, has completed a second recommendation. Of course, it's no guarantee, especially as Percy is trying to talk us all down, but two recommendations don't come around very often, Kane. And they have for you.'

He didn't answer. It was impossible to know what to think, let alone what to say.

'We can have it all, Kane. Our army careers *and* each other.'

'I don't care, you know. I'm happy with my decision to give it up for you. For us.'

'As am I. And maybe we'll still choose to do that one day. But right now that isn't a decision we have to make, so why not take the opportunity being offered?'

She was trembling, he could see it from here. And he'd never wanted so much to take her in his arms and hold her. Kane had no idea how he held himself back. He dropped his hands to brace them on the cool surfaces of the desks, his fingers brushing hers.

She stared at them then back up at him, her expression so charged he thought the air around them should crackle with its intensity.

'It means waiting, though, Matz. We still can't be together until I'm a commissioned officer.'

With another glance down at his hands Mattie slowly—as if it was painful for her to do—lifted her own hands from the desk and took a half-step back.

'We've waited for fourteen years, Kane,' she whispered. 'I think we can wait a little longer.'

'I don't know how,' he growled, forcing himself to take control.

'Neither do I,' Mattie confessed. 'But we'll manage it.'

CHAPTER FOURTEEN

THE OFFICERS' MESS fell silent as Kane's old CO walked the newly commissioned Kane into the room.

Mattie's eyes prickled, hot and stinging, as she watched Kane walk across the room and ring the bell—the invitation for orders allowing every officer to order a drink at the bar, all of which would go on the newly commissioned officer's mess bill at the end of the month.

She watched with incredible patience as he navigated the social waters filled with the many officers who had worked with him over the years and who wanted to congratulate him on his success. And then, at last, people began to drift into groups, and she found herself facing Kane from the other side of the room.

Mattie wasn't sure who moved first, Kane or herself, but suddenly they were standing practically toe to toe, and for the first time ever she could call him Kane in front of anyone, and no one would bat an eyelid.

'Congratulations, *Captain* Wheeler.' She smiled. 'Be grateful it wasn't an official dinner, or they'd have had you popping a champagne bottle with a ceremonial sword.'

'Then I'm glad I got the bell.'

'You won't be when the bill comes.' She chuckled. 'I'll warn you now that first one is a bit of a shocker.'

'I've been warned,' he agreed. 'Still, can I buy you another drink?'

A frisson of excitement rippled through her.

'Actually, I was just going to retire for the evening,' she said clearly, for anyone else around to hear. 'But you can walk me back if you're heading that way.'

'Of course.'

Taking their leave, they walked out of the mess in step but apart. Like any other pair of officers who happened to be leaving together. It was more thrilling than she could have imagined.

'I booked the taxi,' she murmured quietly, when she was sure they were far enough away not to be overheard by anyone.

'I booked the hotel,' he said, and grinned into the night as they headed towards the main gate.

And then they were slipping into the taxi and speeding down the streets, back to the place where it had all pretty much started again only a few months earlier.

'I feel like I'm sixteen again!' Mattie giggled softly, her thighs pressed against Kane's, his arms slung around her shoulders. He dropped his head to her ear and his breath tickled her skin, making her neck goose-bump.

'If we were kids again we'd probably be making out in the back of this cab.'

And, oh, how she was tempted. Long, long months of keeping her distance, just waiting for Kane to finally get his commission. They'd waited so long, and this last leg felt like the longest wait of all.

Now, sliding her hand up the hard ridges of his muscular thigh, she stopped just shy of going too far, delighting in the long breath that Kane hissed out. He dropped his arm down her back, circling his hand around to draw lazy whorls on her hipbone and down to her backside.

'That's unfair,' she protested weakly.

He didn't look remotely repentant.

'Then in future I suggest you don't start something you don't want finished.'

And then they were there, pulling up outside the hotel, and Kane was thrusting a note into the driver's hand and telling him to keep the change.

'In a rush?' she teased.

He cast her a sidelong look.

'Would you prefer me to take my time?'

They could barely keep their hands off each other on the ride up in the lift, grateful for the deserted corridors as they stumbled along, locating their room. And then they were falling through the door and all she could think about was finally, *finally*, reacquainting herself with the body that had made her ache with longing for far too long.

It was the flowers on the bed that stopped her. Pretty lupins, like they'd found in that ruin back during Operation Strikethrough. And on top of them was a distinctive square box.

Her heart caught in her throat.

'Kane? What's going on?'

'Open it and find out,' he told her hoarsely.

Her fingers were trembling as she reached over and took the box. This wasn't what she'd expected, but she couldn't seem to stop herself from imagining. Hoping.

It took her two attempts to open the heavy hinge on the box, and then she thought her legs might buckle beneath her because it wasn't a modern ring, some exquisite, contemporary thing that Kane had scoured jewellery shops for.

This was her mother's ring.

'How…?'

'I asked Hayd's permission to ask for your hand—in lieu of your father.' Kane shrugged. 'He went straight upstairs and brought it down. So I guess you could say he approves.'

She didn't answer him. Especially when he dropped to one knee in front of her.

'So, Mathilda Brigham, after a decade and a half of waiting, of trying to live lives that were never going to be complete without each other, will you do me the honour of marrying me, and making my life whole once again?'

Mattie heard an incoherent sound and it took her a moment to realise it was her. Her chest was still tight and aching, but this time she knew it wasn't because her heart was breaking. It was coming back together, each little shard slipping seamlessly back into place.

Like a little miracle that made her chest swell until she thought it might explode.

'I can't believe this,' she breathed.

Rising up again, Kane cupped her face in his hands and dropped a smooth kiss on her forehead.

'Believe it, Matz.'

She shook her head, swallowing the lump of happiness that was lodged in her throat. Fighting to speak. She gripped his hands and held them in place.

He caught her against him, and she sighed at the way their bodies seem to mould perfectly to each other.

EPILOGUE

THEY WERE MARRIED the following year in the glorious, Grecian-style Guards' Chapel in London's St James's Park, with a uniformed usher trumpeting Mattie's arrival and an honour guard with their arch of swords over the happy couple's departure.

Mattie, walked down the aisle by a delighted Hayden in lieu of her father, had chosen a sleek off-white gown with lace shoulder detailing for modesty, whilst Kane was resplendent in his new officer's uniform.

'I'm still not sure I can believe we get our happy ending,' she whispered as she smoothed her dress in the back seat of the vintage car, and Kane slid in beside her, scooping his willing new wife into his arms.

'It's been a long time coming,' he agreed, his lips brushing hers and instantly setting her body on fire. Making her suddenly wish they didn't have to rush to the hotel to attend the wedding breakfast 'But it *is* finally here. And it's ours to enjoy.'

'Do you think the guests will have time to get to the venue before us?' She affected an air of innocence. 'Or should we give them a little additional time, do you think?'

'Colonel Brigham,' he murmured against her mouth, 'are you suggesting you can't wait?'

'I'm suggesting we've spent years waiting. Today, for

once, is about us finally getting what we've longed for. I don't want to wait any longer.'

'Neither do I,' Kane agreed.

And for the first time in forever they felt as if they had it all. And it felt *right*.

* * * * *